CALL THE ROSTER
OF THE HARD CORPS...

WILLIAM O'NEAL—The baddest and the best. This one-time Green Beret captain picks the wars and calls the shots.

JAMES WENTWORTH III—Proud Oklahoman, well-rounded killer, master of the East's deadliest fighting arts.

JOE FANELLI—Street-corner wiseguy turned demolitions expert, he's far more explosive than his beloved TNT.

STEVE CAINE—Silent lone wolf, who works behind enemy lines with blade, crossbow, and strangler's cord.

JOHN McSHAYNE—Top sergeant, master mechanic, and keeper of the incredible Hard Corps arsenal.

THE HARD CORPS

THE HARD CORPS

CORPS

SLAVE TRADE

CHUCK BAINBRIDGE

JOVE BOOKS, NEW YORK

SLAVE TRADE

A Jove Book/published by arrangement with
the author

PRINTING HISTORY
Jove edition/October 1987

ISBN: 0-515-09211-8

Jove Books are published by The Berkley Publishing Group,
200 Madison Avenue, New York, New York 10016.
The name "JOVE" and the "J" logo
are trademarks belonging to Jove Publications, Inc.

PRINTED IN THE UNITED STATES OF AMERICA

10 9 8 7 6 5 4 3 2 1

CHAPTER 1

THE HARD CORPS followed the motorcycle gang to the roadside gas station and tavern. Here, about six miles east of Lassen Volcanic National Park in Northern California, the run-down little station lay along a lonely strip of dirt road: the sort of place few motorists would ever see, and fewer still would choose to stop at for gas or directions.

A CLOSED sign hung in the window of the gas station. Another sign was posted in the window of the tavern, but nevertheless, it was filled with activity that night. Lights were on inside it and shapes moved across the windows. Loud rock music was playing—punk and heavy metal mostly.

Voices shouted inside the tavern, bellowing to be heard above the blare of the stereo amplifiers. Yet, although laughter mingled with the other noises, very few passers-by would have been tempted to see what the party was like inside the joint. Eleven Harley-Davidson motorcycles were parked in front of the tavern. The choppers were painted black and red. Each bore a symbol of a yellow skull with curved horns and flames jetting from the top of its bony dome.

1

This was the symbol of Lucifer's Wild Riders, a small but notorious outlaw biker gang. The LWR gang had formerly been active in Southern California. The leader, Samuel "Stomper" Torrance, was wanted in Los Angeles for armed robbery, assault and battery, manslaughter, and conspiracy to commit murder. His second-in-command, Fredrick Gordello—a six-foot-four muscle-bound sadist known to his friends as "Gorilla"—was suspected of being involved in most of the crimes Stomper was wanted for, plus a number of sexual assault charges. The other twelve members of the gang—including three women—were also wanted by the police in several jurisdictions in Southern California for crimes that ranged from shoplifting and destruction of private property to rape and murder.

The Lucifer's Wild Riders were as disgusting a collection of scumbags that ever mounted two-wheeler choppers as one could ever hope not to encounter. The cops thought the gang had fled to Oregon or Nevada, but the Hard Corps had discovered the bikers while carrying out surveillance on the Fellowship of Ultimate Living commune.

The FUL was supposed to be a philosophical outfit, a cult of understanding and love for one's fellow human beings. So why the hell were a pack of mad dogs like the Lucifer's Wild Riders connected with the FUL? Either the bikers had completely changed their ways or the cult was a lot more sinister than its public image suggested. After less than a week of surveillance, the Hard Corps were convinced the latter was the truth.

William O'Neal lowered his night-sight binoculars. The Hard Corps had followed the bikers in a U.S. Army surplus jeep. The gang had been easy to track, since their roaring motors could be heard half a mile away. When the Wild Riders finally came to roost at the tavern, the Hard Corps stopped and waited in the darkness almost a mile from the site.

"Has it occurred to you that this is a pretty weird mission for four mercs to take on, Captain?" Joe Fanelli remarked from behind the wheel, chewing the filter end of an unlit cigarette. "I mean, this ain't our usual kind of job."

"No, it isn't," O'Neal agreed as he unlocked the metal footlocker strapped to the back of the jeep. "But the more I've seen of this cult and those cycle-bound savages, the more I think it's the kind of job *somebody* had better take care of, but nobody else seems to be doing shit about. Guess that's why the families hired us. Nothing else has done any good."

James Wentworth III sighed wearily. "Well, what do we do now? Sit here all night watching these evolutionary throwbacks carry on inside that bar, or do we go down and introduce ourselves to the motorcycle maggots?"

"That's pretty good, Lieutenant." Fanelli smiled. "Motorcycle maggots. I like that."

"Hilarious," Steve Caine remarked in his emotionless monotone, a voice that rarely changed to express any sort of feeling. The tall bearded merc's features remained as deadpan as his voice. "How do we handle this, sir?"

"We go in," O'Neal replied as he removed an Uzi submachine gun from the locker. "Don't get careless. Those bikers might be a bunch of scuzzy creeps who never spent any time in the military, let alone the Green Berets, but they're not a group of Sunday School teachers, either. They've all got a history of violence. And police warrants list them as armed and extremely dangerous."

"Their choice in music is certainly obnoxious," Wentworth commented as he reached into the footlocker for his weapons. "How can they stand to listen to that garbage with the volume turned up so loud?"

"Lucky break for us," Caine remarked, setting the bowstring to a flexible bamboo shaft. He gathered up a quiver of hunting arrows and added, "They probably won't hear us approach."

"We could land a 747 next to the tavern and they wouldn't hear us," Wentworth stated as he buckled a gunbelt around his slightly paunchy waist. "It wouldn't be so bad if they played Wagner. Or perhaps Tchaikovsky—"

"Or the Rolling Stones," Fanelli added, working the cocking bolt of his Uzi. "The good stuff they did back in the sixties."

Wentworth made a sour face as if Fanelli's comparison were sacrilege. O'Neal ignored their conversation. Wentworth had been born and raised in an aristocratic Oklahoma oil family and Fanelli was the product of the mean streets of New Jersey. The gentleman-warrior from the South and the tough Italian slum kid from the North seldom agreed on anything, but they'd always get their shit together when it came time to go into action.

The Hard Corps were armed and ready within three minutes. O'Neal and Fanelli carried Uzi submachine guns. Wentworth had assembled an M-16 assault rifle and Caine had a compact MAC-10 Ingram machine pistol for close quarters. He also carried his bow and arrows for silence and long-range shots. Caine had learned his deadly archery skills from the Katu tribesmen in Vietnam. He had, in fact, remained in Vietnam after the American forces withdrew and fought with the Katu against the Communists for almost three years. Caine was an expert in the silent night-fighting skills and camouflage techniques of the Katu, the fiercest and most deadly warriors of the Montagnard tribes.

All four men also carried .45-caliber Colt 1911A1 government-issue autoloading pistols, holstered on their hips. Fanelli also packed a snub-nosed .357 Colt revolver in a holster at the small of his back and a push-button NATO knife in his pocket. Caine's knife was a survival-fighting knife with a six-inch blade in a leather sheath on his hip.

Wentworth carried the most unusual bladed weapon. A *wakazashi* sword was thrust in his belt. The handle of the samurai short sword was at navel level, in position for a lightning-fast cross draw. Wentworth was an expert in *ken-jutsu*, the most aggressive form of Japanese fencing.

The Lucifer's Wild Riders weren't expecting trouble. They hadn't posted a sentry outside the tavern. Obviously, the outlaw bikers felt perfectly safe in their remote party site. But the four Hard Corps mercenaries didn't take anything for granted. They approached slowly, cautiously, with weapons held ready. None of the bikers seemed to be outside.

O'Neal gestured for Caine to move to one of the windows and pointed at Fanelli, cutting a small circle with his index finger. Both men nodded. Caine headed for the window while Fanelli crept to the back of the building. O'Neal moved to the front door while Wentworth checked the gas station to make certain it was empty.

The Hard Corps commander listened at the door. The music was uncomfortably loud, but he heard lots of voices inside. Except for an occassional shouted obscenity, few words were clear. O'Neal heard a lot of laughter and slurred, drunken yelling.

Caine peered through the window. He saw a number of motorcycle hoods dressed in leather jackets and ragged vests. A lot of them wore beards and untrimmed mustaches. Some wore spike-studded bracelets, or thick steel chains for necklaces. Almost all wore some form of headgear, which included straw cowboy hats, caps, and helmets—football helmets, steel military helmets with Nazi swastikas or the LWR emblem painted on them; one guy even had a reproduction of a Viking helmet, with two great curved horns jutting from the crown—but none wore regular motorcycle headgear.

One of the female members was sprawled across a pool table, stark naked with a bare-assed male on top of her. Another horny cycle bum was standing in line with his pants down, waiting for his turn. More bikers were seated at tables, guzzling pitchers of beer or bottles of Jack Daniel's. Some seemed to be smoking reefer.

Another female biker was lying on the floor with a slobbering male goon pumping his naked butt as he sprawled across her. The woman gazed up at the ceiling, chewing a wad of gum, apparently bored with the routine coupling. Only a handful of bikers watched these antics with any interest.

Two shaggy morons were throwing knives at a dart

board mounted on a wall. The knives generally missed the target and failed to stick when they did. Caine smiled and shook his head at the clumsiness of the knife throwers. The dummies were trying to use switchblades and cheap Bowies as if they were throwing knives. The knives bounced off the wall and hit the floor. The blade to a switch-knife snapped in two on impact. The drunken dolts giggled and continued to throw knives as if determined to ruin every blade they could lay their shaky, dirty hands on.

Wentworth approached O'Neal. He held up a hand, thumb and forefinger touching to signal "OK." O'Neal nodded and turned to Caine. The tall bearded merc nodded and drew an arrow from the quiver strapped to his back. He notched the arrow to the bowstring. O'Neal pointed at Caine and nodded.

Caine drew back the arrow and aimed at the window. He released the arrow and fired it through the glass pane. The missile slammed into the dart board, nailing the bull's-eye with the steel tip of the arrowhead.

"What the fuck!" a confused voice snorted.

"I didn't throw it, man," another voice yelled.

"Robin Hood strikes again," O'Neal muttered as he slammed a boot into the door just below the knob.

The lock exploded on impact and O'Neal charged inside. He literally ran into a startled and very drunk biker and slammed the frame of his Uzi into the man's hairy face. The Lucifer's Wild Rider slumped to the floor in a dazed heap as O'Neal swung his Uzi toward the remaining gang members. He stepped forward. Gasps of astonishment mingled with the painfully loud music. The bikers backed away. One of the women screamed. The goons who had been busy with the other females tried to pull up their pants and move away at the same time. One man failed to accomplish this and tripped over his own trousers.

James Wentworth entered, stepping behind O'Neal. He aimed his M-16 at the jukebox and fired a quick three-round burst into the machine. The high-velocity 5.56-mm slugs smashed plastic and metal, bursting apart the eight-track cassette tape inside the carriage. The heavy-metal music came to an abrupt halt.

"Thank God." Wentworth sighed with relief.

"What the hell is this shit?" a tall man with long limbs and sleek muscles demanded, pulling a pair of mirror-lensed sunglasses from his face to display his fierce emerald-green eyes.

O'Neal recognized him from the computer dot-matrix replica of a mug shot he'd seen. The mug shot had accompanied a copy of the police record John McShayne had gotten from a tap into the LAPD memory banks. Samuel Torrance had grown a bandido mustache and his hair was a little longer since the mug shot had been taken, but O'Neal still recognized the leader of the motorcycle gang.

"Stomper" looked as mean as a cornered cobra. The checkered grips of a .38-caliber revolver jutted from Torrance's belt, but he wasn't dumb enough to reach for the piece with an Uzi pointed at his belly. He stood with his back to the bar, the heels of his palms resting on the counter. If Stomper was scared, he did a good job at hiding it.

The second-in-command of the Lucifer's Wild Riders stood beside Torrance. Fredrick Gordello was a big, ugly brute with a broad nose that had been broken and bent out of shape. His face was framed by matted black hair and a thick, ragged beard. The "Gorilla" wore a leather jacket. He didn't wear a shirt, probably because he liked to display his hairy, muscular chest. Gordello's arms were coiled with thick muscles, as if he carried pet pythons under his skin.

"Who the fuck are you cocksuckers?" the Gorilla demanded. He spoke as if using language were an uncommon task and a burden for his limited intellect.

Gordello wasn't very bright, but it didn't take an Einstein to see that two guys armed with automatic weapons were a serious threat. O'Neal and Wentworth wouldn't have impressed him if they weren't carrying guns. The Hard Corps commander was a big, husky guy, but not nearly as big as the Gorilla. He was also ten years older than the twenty-eight-year-old biker thug. But O'Neal's rugged features and hard blue eyes revealed he was a genuine hardcase and wouldn't hesitate to blow a hole through anybody who pissed him off.

The Gorilla had an even lower opinion of Wentworth. The merc lieutenant appeared to be a few years older than O'Neal, although Wentworth was actually a year younger than the Hard Corps commander. Wentworth was thicker around the waist than O'Neal and his hair was balding at the top. Gordello thought Wentworth looked ridiculous dressed in tiger-stripe camouflage fatigues and paratrooper boots. The uniform suited O'Neal, but Gordello thought Wentworth looked like one of those over-the-hill clerks who try to play war games on the weekend. The samurai sword in Wentworth's belt seemed like the ultimate stupidity to the Gorilla.

While O'Neal aimed his weapon at the two gang leaders, Wentworth covered the other cycle hoods with his M-16. However, the scrawny, ratlike bartender behind the counter seemed to have been overlooked. He stood behind Gordillo and reached under the counter for a sawed-off Savage 12-gauge shotgun.

"Try it and I'll splatter you all over this dump," Joe Fanelli warned as he entered through the back door and jabbed the barrel of his Uzi into the small of the bartender's back.

"Oh, shit," the guy rasped, stiffening as the hard metal cylinder pressed against his spine. "I give, man. You got me cold—"

He whirled suddenly and tried to knock aside Fanelli's weapon and wrestle it from the mercenary's grasp. The trick might have worked with a less experienced or untrained opponent, but Fanelli was familiar with the technique. The tough guy from Jersey quickly jerked his Uzi away from the bartender's slashing arms and immediately drove the metal stock of the submachine gun into the ratman's chest.

The blow knocked him back against the bar. The guy

gasped as his breath rushed from his lungs. Fanelli drove another butt stroke to the bartender's lower abdomen. The man doubled up with a choking groan and Fanelli quickly slammed a knee into his opponent's face. The bartender fell to the floor, blood oozing from his bashed-in mouth.

"Your bartender's sleeping on the job!" Fanelli announced, glancing down at the unconscious man. "Guess I'll take over now. I'll see if I can't mix up some nice drinks for you boys."

The wiry Italian from Jersey grabbed a whiskey bottle from a shelf behind the bar. At one time, Fanelli would have been happy to drink the whole bottle by himself, but he'd realized he was an alcoholic, and he'd been on the wagon for years. True, he *had* slipped during the Hard Corps' last mission, in Bolivia. What the hell, he figured. Nobody's perfect.

He grabbed the bottle by the neck and hurled it across the room with the same accuracy that had made him a valuable pitcher at stickball as a kid and an accomplished grenade thrower as a soldier in 'Nam. The bottle smashed into a pitcher of beer on a table. Glass exploded and liquid splashed the startled bikers near the table.

"Jesus!" one screamed, covering his face in fear that flying glass might get in his eyes.

"Naw," Fanelli replied cheerfully. "I'm just Joseph."

A Lucifer's Wild Rider suddenly reached for a .22 pistol at the small of his back. Steve Caine saw through the window and launched another arrow. The biker convulsed with pain as the sharp tip of the missile pierced his neck. The feathered butt jutted from one side of his neck and the crimson-stained broadhead protruded from the opposite side. The goon half-turned and wilted to the floor.

Two other morons ducked behind a table and turned it over for shelter. One guy reached for a compact .380 pistol in his boot. Wentworth aimed his M-16 and fired six rounds through the flimsy tabletop. The bullets punched through plywood as if it were paper and drilled into the chest of one biker, bursting his heart with a double dose of 5.56-mm lead poisoning.

The other man tumbled on his side, both arms clutching his bullet-ravaged stomach. He howled in agony until Wentworth shot him with two more M-16 rounds. The biker's face split open and his brains poured out onto the floor. The rest of the gang jumped back. Several pressed their backs against a wall and held their hands overhead. The two naked women cringed in a corner, their arms held high, unconcerned that their bare breasts jiggled and bobbed. Everyone was too preoccupied to look them over.

"Don't try it, Torrance," O'Neal warned when he noticed the leader's hand had moved toward the gun in his belt.

"Take it easy," Stomper urged, using thumb and forefinger to ease the .38 from his belt. He dropped it to the floor and kicked the gun toward O'Neal. "Okay?"

"Nice start," the Hard Corps commander replied as he stepped closer. "Now, suppose you tell us about the Fellowship of Ultimate Living."

"Shit, fella," Torrance said with a nervous smile. "Do I look like a fuckin' Hare Krishna or somethin'?"

"You look like a piece of shit who's committed enough crimes to deserve a bullet in the gut so you can whimper your confessions as you bleed to death," O'Neal answered. "I know who you are and what you are. I don't really give a damn if I have to kill you or not."

"You wanna arrest me, pig?" Stomper asked. "Go ahead, but I ain't sayin' shit until I get my lawyer—"

O'Neal kicked him suddenly in the nuts. Stomper gasped in agony. His eyes swelled and he doubled up and fell to his knees. The biker's mouth seemed frozen in a small, tight oval shape as he clutched his battered genitals with both hands.

"You're gonna talk, you bastard," O'Neal stated. "If you don't, I'll kill you right here and now. One of your boys can answer my questions instead. Doesn't mean shit to me who talks or how many of you assholes I have to kill to get an answer."

He slammed a boot into Torrance and kicked the biker into the base of the bar. Stomper slid and landed on his ass. O'Neal stepped back and aimed his Uzi at the biker's face.

"Your decision, Stomper," he said in a hard voice. "Make it quick, 'cause I don't intend to hang around here all night."

"What kinda pricks are you guys?" Gordello demanded, furious that he was unable to protect his boss.

"The kind that will blow your brainless head off if you don't shut up," Wentworth warned.

"Fuck you, baldy," the Gorilla snapped. "If you didn't have that gun I'd fuck you over with one arm tied behind my back."

"You can use both hands," Wentworth said with a smile. "But you have to agree to tell us everything you know if I win. Will you agree to those terms? Or are you too stupid to understand what I said?"

"You ain't gonna win," Gordello sneered. "I'm gonna break your fuckin' back, old man."

"Lieutenant," O'Neal said with reproach in the tone of his voice. "This isn't the time for this sort of thing."

"Might save us some time, Captain," Wentworth stated. "Would you hold on to my rifle?"

"Okay," O'Neal reluctantly agreed, taking the M-16.

"You carrying any weapons, apeshit?" Wentworth asked Gordello. "I imagine trying to use a gun would be too complicated for you. Trying to aim a weapon and work a trigger would probably tax your Neanderthal brain too much. Maybe you have a club. Something heavy and simple."

Gordello reached under his hobnail-studded vest and removed a mallet with a rubber-coated sledge. He placed the hammer on the counter. Wentworth nodded as if to say "I told you so" and took the *wakazashi* from his belt.

A pair of Lucifer's Wild Riders noticed that Wentworth had stepped between them and O'Neal. The bikers decided

to make their move. Confident O'Neal wouldn't open fire
and risk hitting one of his own men, the pair tried to jump
Wentworth from behind. One held a beer bottle in his fist
and raised it overhead as a club. The other drew a large
Bowie knife from a sheath at the small of his back.

Joe Fanelli saw the guy pull the knife and promptly
nailed him with a trio of Uzi slugs. The high-powered
9-mm parabellums smashed into the biker's chest and sent
his corpse hurtling backward to collapse against several of
his teammates.

Wentworth grabbed the handle of his samurai short
sword with one hand and yanked the scabbard off with the
other. He began to turn to face the second attacker even
before the naked steel had cleared its sheath. The long,
curved metal rose to block the beer bottle in the biker's
fist.

Sharp steel struck the guy's wrist. It severed skin and
muscle and cleaved through bone. The biker screamed as
the beer bottle shattered on the floor. His severed hand was
still clutching the neck of the bottle. Wentworth immediately followed the sword slash with a deadly thrust. The
sharp point pierced the man's solar plexus and stabbed upward into his heart.

"Oh, fuck," Gordello rasped. Suddenly he didn't find
Wentworth's sword the slightest bit amusing.

"Be right with you, walnut-brain," Wentworth remarked, grunting from exertion as he yanked the *wakazashi* blade from the man's lifeless flesh.

"You ain't gonna use that toad-sticker on me?" the Gorilla asked, his voice almost pleading. "Are you?"

"Of course not," the merc lieutenant assured him. He
suddenly snapped his wrist and flicked blood from the
blade. Crimson splattered Gordello's broad face.
"Wouldn't be fair, would it?"

Wentworth placed the sword on the floor next to the
scabbard. Gordello wiped the blood from his face with his
palm. The big man was trembling with rage. Wentworth's
tactics had unnerved him, but the Gorilla still figured he

could take the mercenary if Wentworth didn't have the sword. After all, Gordello was six inches taller than Wentworth, at least ten years younger, and he outweighed the older man by more than thirty pounds. Not flabby pounds, either. Gordello had lots of muscle, and he wasn't soft around the middle like Wentworth. *Shit,* he thought. *Kicking the shit out of baldy will be a cinch.*

"Hey, he still has a gun!" a biker declared, noticing the Colt pistol on Wentworth's hip.

"It'll stay in the holster if none of you other clowns get involved," Wentworth assured the others. He turned to face Gordello. "I'm waiting, lobotomy-head."

"Shit!" the Gorilla growled as he charged forward.

The big man feinted a left jab and swung a roundhouse right cross at Wentworth's head. It was a clumsy attack, but Gordello seldom needed to hit an opponent more than once. If he could score a single solid punch at Wentworth's head he was sure he could knock it right off the bastard's shoulders.

But his fist missed its target. Wentworth dodged the punch and quickly grabbed the Gorilla's wrist and elbow. He pulled with one hand, pushed with the other, and dropped to one knee. Gordello's forward momentum went out of control and he found himself sliding head-over-heels. The biker crashed to the floor hard. Gasps of surprise filled the tavern. The Lucifer's Wild Riders could barely believe they had actually seen Wentworth toss the Gorilla across the room.

"It's all in the leverage," Wentworth announced as Gordello started to rise from the floor. "Care to see some more?"

"Quit fuckin' around with him, Jim," O'Neal said with annoyance. This was no time for showing off. "Just take the son of a bitch out."

Gordello approached Wentworth more carefully this time. He held his balled fists at chest level and slowly started to pace in a circle around Wentworth, trying to plan a better attack. The merc waited for him to make the next move. Wentworth's hands were open, one arm extended and the other held at solar plexus level.

The Gorilla tried another technique he liked, a standard move among street fighters. He swung a kick for Wentworth's groin. The merc chopped the side of his hand across Gordello's shin bone. The biker cursed and swung a fist at Wentworth. The Hard Corps lieutenant ducked under the wild punch and rammed his knuckles under the larger man's rib cage.

Gordello groaned and Wentworth hit him in the side of the head with a heel-of-the-palm stroke. The Gorilla staggered from the blow and swung a backfist at Wentworth. The merc caught his opponent's arm at the wrist and elbow again.

James Wentworth III was a fourth-dan black belt in *aikido*, a Japanese martial art little known and largely misunderstood in the West. He was skilled in the throws, locks and holds, *atemi* striking techniques, and the stick and sword maneuvers taught to advanced students of the art. Wentworth could have used any of a hundred techniques after he seized the Gorilla's arm, but he decided to put the big man out of action fast.

He stomped a boot heel into Gordello's instep and twisted the biker's wrist. His left hand shoved on the Gorilla's elbow to lock the limb in a straight-arm-bar hold. Gordello doubled up from the pressure applied to his shoulder and trapped arm. Wentworth swung a leg over the biker's hunched back and jammed his buttocks into Gordello's shoulder. He pulled the captive arm between his legs and sat on the guy's shoulder, driving the Gorilla to the floor.

Gordello landed on his belly, helplessly pinned by his opponent. Wentworth kept the biker's elbow locked and applied pressure with both hands to Gordello's wrist. Bones in the joint popped in response. The Gorilla howled in agony.

"That's just because you're a disgusting brute and a

rapist," Wentworth declared as he applied pressure to the elbow. "Now, are you going to talk?"

"Fuck you!" Gordello cried in anger and pain.

Wentworth neatly broke his elbow. The Gorilla shrieked and tried buck the mercenary off his back, but Wentworth pulled back on the arm and braced his butt against the man's shoulder. He twisted hard and heard the joint crunch. Wentworth had dislocated the Gorilla's shoulder. Fredrick Gordello uttered a soft whimper and passed out.

"I don't think he'll tell us much, after all," Wentworth commented sadly. "Maybe I can revive him . . ."

"Forget it," O'Neal muttered, pointing his Uzi at Samuel Torrance. He held the M-16 by its barrel. "Come here and get your rifle. I'm tired of wasting time with these idiots. We're either gonna get some answers or we'll start killin' 'em off one by one . . ."

"You've already killed five of my men, you fuckin' bastard!" Torrance snarled as he climbed to his feet, leaning against the bar with one hand and rubbing his balls with the other.

Fanelli leaned across the counter and swatted the back of his hand across the biker's face. Torrance slid along the bar and nearly fell, but managed to stay upright.

"Watch your mouth, fella," Fanelli told him. "Let's discuss this like civilized chappies. Right-o?"

Stomper placed a hand to his face and nodded. Then he suddenly swung a right cross at Fanelli's face. The wiry merc's lightning reflexes blocked the punch. He raised the Uzi in front of his face and Torrance rammed his fist into the steel frame of the submachine gun. The biker gasped in pain when he broke a knuckle on the hard metal.

"That's not how it's done," Fanelli commented and swung a hard left hook to Stomper's jaw. "See?"

The punch spun Torrance around and O'Neal hit him under the heart with a karate chop. Stomper fell against the bar and dropped on his ass again. Blood dripped from his mouth as he coughed hard and stared up at O'Neal with defeated, tear-coated eyes.

"Okay," Torrance said, struggling to catch his breath. "You win. What do you want to know about Glover and the cult? You guys sure ain't cops. What you want? A piece of the action?"

"Just tell us what your gang does for the cult," O'Neal answered, his voice gentle. He could see that Stomper's spirit had broken. The gang had been rendered helpless, Stomper's toughest man defeated in hand-to-hand combat; and now Stomper's own life hung by a frayed thread.

O'Neal was a natural leader of men, and that meant he understood them better than most. Stomper had been stunned by the totality of the attack. He didn't need more threats or physical abuse.

"You want a drink? A cigarette?" O'Neal murmured.

"Both," Stomper said with a nod.

"Pour the man a drink," O'Neal told Fanelli. "A nice strong one. Whiskey okay?"

"Sure," Torrance assured him. He swallowed the whiskey in one gulp and caught his breath. "Well, you know there's a lot more to the Fellowship of Ultimate Living than a bunch of kids following a guy from Australia. You know about the dope and the girls, right?"

"Refresh my memory," O'Neal answered, not admitting that he wasn't aware that the cult was involved in drugs. *And what does Torrance mean by "the girls"?*

"Well," Torrance began as Fanelli handed him another glass of whiskey. "We make the deals with the dealers. You know, the big dudes. Coke, horse, crack. The dealers need mules. Kids without criminal records who look clean-cut and conservative make the best mules. We're just kind of a go-between for the cult and the dealers."

"Sonofabitch," Fanelli muttered with disgust.

"These kids do this willingly?" O'Neal inquired as he tossed a cigarette to Stomper and lit one for himself.

"Christ," Stomper replied as he leaned forward to accept the flame from O'Neal's Zippo to get his cigarette going. "Those kids *don't have* any will by the time Glover gets done with them."

"What's he use on 'em?" Fanelli asked. "Drugs?"

"Dunno," Torrance answered. "Drugs, brainwashing, hypnosis, black magic; I don't know a whole lot, but he sure fucks 'em up mentally. They're all fuckin' wacko. You know, they're scared shitless of Glover, but they still worship the ground he walks on. Weirder'n shit."

"Tell us about the girls," O'Neal said grimly.

"What else do you do with girls?" Torrance said with a shrug. "They got pussies, you make a lot of money with 'em."

"You talking about white slavery?" Fanelli asked, surprise obvious in the tone of his voice. "I thought that shit was out with the sultans and the opium dens."

"Think again, bright boy," Stomper declared. "If you can supply the right kind of girls to the right sources, you can make a bundle hustlin' ass. Girls're always girls, guys always guys. Blondes are the big demands, I think, mostly south of the border."

"Glover is selling girls to brothels in Mexico?" O'Neal frowned. "I don't follow you. How the hell does he get them there?"

"Ever hear of the Mexican Mafia?" Toorrance said with a shrug. "Well, them greaser gangsters got connections all over Central America. Guatemala, Honduras, maybe even still in Nicaragua. Got the Mex Mafia here in the U.S., too, man. The Mexican mob works kinda in agreement with the big coke gangs in South America. Those girls Glover sends down there could wind up anywhere. Not just Mexico City or Tijuana."

"And you're the go-between for Glover and the mob," O'Neal said in a hard voice. "I guess you must have made a lot of connections with dope dealers and pimps over your long career."

"If we hadn't done it somebody else would have," Stomper said with a helpless shrug.

"Too bad for you it wasn't somebody else," O'Neal remarked.

"Wh-What you gonna do?" Torrance was scared now,

scared worse than he had been before. "You can't just kill us . . ."

He suddenly hurled his glass at O'Neal's face, but the Hard Corps commander dodged it easily. Some whiskey splashed his shirt and cheek, but missed his eyes. Stomper started to lunge toward him. The merc leader's boot shot out and caught the biker in the side of the face and knocked him to the floor.

Some of the other bikers saw this as a signal to make their move. One of the guys who fancied himself a knife-thrower grabbed a Bowie knife from the floor and cocked his arm for a throw. A half-wit with a Nazi helmet grabbed a snub-nosed revolver one of his slain buddies had dropped. Another biker dived for a duffle bag to try to draw a sawed-off 16-gauge shotgun from the container. One of the female bikers produced a diminutive .25-caliber pistol from somewhere. This was quite a feat considering she was still stark naked.

"Stupid!" Wentworth shouted, angry with the woman for forcing him to open fire on her, which ordinarily was against his code of honor.

He triggered the M-16 and shot the pistol-packing woman between her bouncing breasts. Three 5.56-mm bullets ruined her ripe beauty forever and tore into her heart. The woman fell back into a wall and slumped lifeless to the floor.

The knife artist and the biker with the revolver were both located near the far end of the room. They felt they were more difficult targets for the three mercenaries near the bar. They had either forgotten about Steve Caine or assumed the merc outside the window was only armed with a bow and arrows.

Steve Caine showed them how wrong they were, but neither man lived to learn much from the lesson. The mercenary opened fire with his MAC-10. A volley of 9-mm bullets blasted the window into flying glass shards and chunks of shattered framework.

The knife-thrower caught two parabellum slugs through

the side of his head. His skull burst open and he collapsed to the floor, another slab of worthless dead meat. The creep with the revolver turned toward the window and lived long enough to see the muzzle flash of Caine's Ingram before 9-mm rounds smashed through his face and drilled three lethal tunnels through his brain.

Joe Fanelli, meanwhile, spotted the biker who had yanked the single-barrel shotgun from the duffle bag. The merc from Jersey blasted the cretin with a burst of Uzi slugs. Bullets ripped into the biker's upper chest and sent him tumbling backward over a table. The guy pulled the trigger to his shotgun as he fell. The cut-down cannon bellowed and discharged a load of buckshot into another Lucifer's Wild Rider, who had been standing near the wall with his hands raised in surrender. His upper torso dissolved in a bloodied pulped mess and he dropped lifeless to the floor.

The biker loonie with the Viking helmet panicked and grabbed a chair and raised it overhead like an oversized club. O'Neal clucked his tongue with disgust and shot him with a three-round burst of 9-mm Uzi projectiles. The horned helmet clattered on the floor and its owner landed on top of it. The sharp horns pierced his back. One stabbed under his left shoulder blade into his heart.

"These cocksuckers have got to be the stupidest bunch of bastards I've seen in a long time," Fanelli commented. "We didn't even get to take 'em outside."

"I know," O'Neal said with a sigh. They had originally captured fifteen prisoners for questioning and now they only had four. "This doesn't seem to be the best place to talk to them. Let's move 'em."

"I'll wake up the Gorilla," Wentworth declared as he approached Gordello's prone figure. The big biker was already beginning to stir.

"Tell Steve we're gonna corral these jokers outside," O'Neal told Wentworth. "Tell him to watch them when they file out the door. If any of them try to run, Steve should shoot at their legs. We don't want to kill any more of these characters."

Wentworth nodded. He understood the problem. So far they couldn't turn over any information to the Federal authorities, or even give an anonymous phone call to the police. Taping confessions under duress would be inadmissible in court, so the bikers' information would be worthless unless it produced leads to solid evidence against the Fellowship of Ultimate Living.

The Hard Corps was involved in a field that wasn't their area of expertise anyway. They were mercenaries, not private investigators, not government agents or even vigilantes. However, nobody else had been able to learn much about the cult. When the Hard Corps had been hired, they'd decided to do what they did best.

They were going to war against Glover and the Fellowship of Ultimate Living.

Every good commander tries to learn as much about the enemy as possible. So far, the Hard Corps hadn't been able to find out much about what the cult was up to . . . until slimy Stomper Torrance had opened his mouth about the drugs and white slavery. The story could be bullshit, but Torrance didn't seem like a man with a lot of imagination. Still, they needed to cross-check Stomper's claims by questioning the other members of the gang—which had been reduced to Gordello, the two surviving women, and the rat-faced bartender who wasn't really even part of the gang.

They herded the survivors out the door. Caine covered the bikers with his MAC-10 as they stepped outside with O'Neal and Wentworth right behind them. Fanelli moved to the window to climb outside and assist Caine.

He was the first to see the station wagon roll to a halt on the road. The headlights were not lit and the vehicle had apparently cruised downhill without using its engine. Car doors opened and four men emerged with long-barreled weapons in their hands.

"Steve!" Fanelli rasped harshly.

"I see them," Caine replied as he slipped into the shadows.

Fanelli wasn't sure who the strangers were. They might be lawmen of some sort, or hunters. Or they might be something else. He moved across the barroom to warn O'Neal and Wentworth. However, the Hard Corps officers had already spotted the newcomers. It was too dark to determine who they were, but the mercenaries sensed danger. The sixth sense of advanced survival rang a warning inside their heads.

"Get down!" O'Neal shouted even before he saw the gunmen aim their weapons at the prisoners.

Caine had already vanished into the dark, but Stomper Torrance, Gorilla Gordello, the two biker women, and the ratty little bartender weren't quick enough. The newcomers opened fire with an assortment of weapons. At least two men used automatic rifles, large-caliber weapons from the sound of the roaring gunshots. One guy fired a shotgun with solid slugs instead of buckshot.

Torrance received three big bullet holes across the chest. Blood dripped from the gory exit wounds in his back as the leader of the Lucifer's Wild Riders wilted to the ground. The Gorilla's upper torso exploded from a .50-caliber "deerslayer" shotgun slug. His corpse fell into the bartender as another barrage of automatic fire cut down the two women.

O'Neal and Wentworth returned fire from the edge of the doorway. Bullets raked the mysterious gunmen. One of the riflemen doubled up, clutching his gut-shot belly. The other three fired at the building as they retreated toward the station wagon. O'Neal and Wentworth ducked while splinters spewed from the doorway and plaster burst from the walls.

Fanelli fired his Uzi from the window. One of the gunmen spun about, hit somewhere in the upper body by one or more parabellum slugs. His shotgun-toting partner returned fire. A big .50-caliber lead projectile blasted a hole as big as a baby's fist in the wall next to the window. Fanelli dropped to the floor.

"Sonofabitch," he muttered, wishing he had a hand grenade.

Steve Caine had crept unseen to the side of the building. He had ample cover, but the Ingram MAC-10 was a short-range weapon and the enemy were too far away to fire accurately at the trio with the machine pistol. Caine notched an arrow to his bow and launched the missile. It hit the shotgunner in the general area of the solar plexus. The gunman dropped his weapon and staggered backward. The curare-laced arrow insured that the man would die from poison even if the wound itself was not lethal. He collapsed face-first in the grass.

Only one gunsel hadn't been hit by Hard Corps projectiles. He suddenly pulled a blunt pistollike device and aimed it at the gas station. He pulled the trigger and a brilliant orange comet streaked from the muzzle. The flare hit the gas pumps. The hot projectile ignited the fuel tanks and the gas pumps exploded with fiery rage. Flaming gasoline splashed the stationhouse and the building was instantly ablaze.

The gunman took advantage of the distraction to flee to the station wagon. He slid behind the wheel as his wounded comrade staggered toward the car. The driver allowed the injured man to reach the car door before he shot him in the face. The station wagon engine roared to life and the vehicle rolled into reverse.

Wentworth fired his M-16 at the windshield. Bullets pierced glass and formed a cracked pattern in the window, but the driver continued to retreat. The station wagon spun into a wild turn and rocketed up the road from the battlefield. Wentworth triggered his rifle and a few 5.56-mm rounds chased the fleeing wagon. If they found their target, it didn't matter because the vehicle continued to bolt up the road.

"Forget it," O'Neal told Wentworth. "He's gone."

"We going after him?" the lieutenant asked.

"Doubt if we'd catch him," the Hard Corps commander replied as he removed a spent magazine from his Uzi. "That car has a souped-up engine and the driver handled it like a pro. Bastard probably knows these roads a lot better than we do. Just be a waste of time."

"Did you see that asshole gun down his own partner?" Fanelli asked, more a statement of astonishment than a real question. "Poor guy's wounded and that prick kills him instead of giving him a ride."

"That 'poor guy' was one of the people trying to kill us," Wentworth said dryly.

"Shit, Lieutenant," Fanelli growled. "You know what I mean, damn it. Why'd that fucker kill him?"

"If he hadn't killed him," O'Neal began, "he would have had to take the wounded man to a hospital. Gunshot wounds are reported to the police. He killed the guy to maintain security."

"Which means none of them were carrying any sort of I.D., so there's no point in searching them," Wentworth added.

"Check anyway," O'Neal stated. "Maybe one of them was careless. Might have an engraved wristwatch or old dog tags. Never know."

"Figure those button men were working for Glover?" Caine inquired as he approached the other mercs.

"Probably," O'Neal answered. "But I doubt that we'll be able to prove it. We've got to get the hell out of here, too. We've committed enough felonies to wind up in a California state prison for a couple of lifetimes. We'd have a lot of trouble convincing the cops that we're really the good guys."

"That depends on your point of view," Wentworth remarked.

Fanelli groaned. "Fuck you, Lieutenant."

"Save the pillow talk for later," O'Neal barked, reaching for his cigarettes. "We've got a lot to do before the night's over. Tomorrow we've gotta see our employers and

I'm not looking forward to telling them how this mission has gone so far."

"We've made some progress, sir," Caine remarked.

"I don't think the parents of those kids are going to look at it that way," O'Neal stated. "How do you think you'd feel if you found out your son or daughter was not only hooked up with a crackpot cult, but probably a drug addict as well? Not to mention the fact that Stomper said a lot of the girls were being sold into some kind of white slavery and shipped out of the country."

"This job is getting ugly," Wentworth commented.

"Ugly?" O'Neal snorted. "It's goddamn hideous."

CHAPTER 2

CAROL HENDERSON LISTENED SILENTLY as O'Neal and Wentworth explained what had happened at the tavern. The tall, slender woman with prematurely gray hair closed her eyes and shook her head sadly. The situation was even worse than she'd suspected.

Donald Baskin didn't take the bad news so calmly. The beefy, middle-aged shoe store manager hammered a fist on Carol's coffee table. His broad face was purple with rage as he glared up at O'Neal and Wentworth.

"In other words," Baskin bellowed in his deep, Alabama-born voice, "you boys blew it! We're supposed to pay y'all fifty thousand dollars to get our kids back, and you go get yore-selves into a barroom brawl with a bunch o' motorcycle trash!"

"We already explained how the Lucifer's Wild Riders were connected with Glover's cult," Wentworth replied, his tone calm and controlled. "It was a valid lead that revealed information about the Fellowship of Ultimate Living. We realized the motorcycle gang had to be connected with some sort of criminal activity concerning the cult, but we didn't know at the time what that involved."

"And you can't learn nothin' else about Glover's outfit 'cause you up and killed the motorcycle gang," Baskin complained. "What the hell you think we're payin' you for, son? See how many people you can kill? We ain't payin' you for corpses. We want our kids back, right now!"

"Donald," Carol said in a quiet firm voice. "Please, try to calm down. We're all upset."

"Some of us are probably more upset than others," Baskin snapped. "Your daughter's already dead, Carol. You ain't really got that much to lose, do you?"

"Donald!" Roberta Kelton said sharply. "That was a terrible thing to say. Carol's as concerned about stopping Glover and his awful cult as any of us."

"I'm sorry, Carol," Baskin replied. "Guess I'm just frustrated."

O'Neal could understand that. The Hard Corps had been hired a week ago to deal with the Fellowship of Ultimate Living and they were frustrated, too. The FUL kept a low profile and presented a public image that seemed reasonably benevolent. Yet the mercenaries were finding evidence that the FUL was far more sinister than it appeared. The problem was, they couldn't prove it.

The Hard Corps had never even heard of the Fellowship of Ultimate Living before Dave Colton contacted them and suggested they meet with Carol Henderson. Colton was an ex-Green Beret who'd known the Hard Corps in 'Nam. He'd settled down after the war, got a job with the Veterans' Administration, and raised a family. He'd adjusted to civilian life, but he still kept in touch with the Hard Corps. The mercenaries trusted Colton's judgment so they agreed to meet with the Henderson woman.

Carol's nineteen-year-old daughter had joined the FUL. Six months later she sent her mother a letter from Phoenix, Arizona. The girl claimed she'd left the cult more than a month earlier, but she was financially in trouble and asked Carol to send her money by Western Union to a branch office in Phoenix. Carol obliged. Two more letters arrived.

None had a return address, but both requested money to be sent in the same manner.

Then Carol received a telegram from the Phoenix Police Department. They asked her to come to Arizona to identify a young woman's body believed to be that of Donna Henderson. Carol flew to Phoenix and confirmed that the dead girl was indeed her daughter. Donna's skin was marked by needle tracks; she had died of an overdose of heroin. The condition of some of the needle scars suggested she had been taking drugs for several months. The police were satisfied that Donna was just another dumb junkie who'd accidentally OD'd.

Carol Henderson wasn't willing to accept that. She was convinced that the Fellowship of Ultimate Living was responsible for her daughter's death. She contacted the parents of other kids who'd joined the FUL. Many, it turned out, had similar stories to tell. Some of the parents had lost their children forever. Like Donna, other FUL kids had died from drug overdoses, automobile accidents, alleged suicide, or simply disappeared. None of these incidents could be directly connected with the cult, since the dead or missing young people had all supposedly left it at least a month before they died or vanished.

The police in several states had been contacted by distraught parents, but they could do little to confirm these accusations. Most were inclined to assume any kid who got mixed up with a cult was mentally unbalanced in the first place, so they weren't too surprised that some former members of the FUL became junkies after they left the cult. They figured these kids were all social misfits anyway. Stupid brats probably wound up on the streets after they left the cult and got themselves killed due to their own stupidity or weakness. The cops were also inclined to regard the parents as whimpering hypocrites. After all, they reasoned, if the parents had brought up their kids right, they wouldn't have joined a goddamn cult.

The parents had tried everything. They had filled out petitions to have the cult investigated. Local and state authorities visited the California chapter of the Fellowship of Ultimate Living and found nothing to merit the parents' claims of misconduct. They had tried to interest the media in their plight, but their evidence was circumstantial and none of the news personnel wanted to risk a lawsuit by prying into the cult's activities. Besides, cults weren't major news items anymore.

So finally, Carol and the other parents had reached their last resort—the Hard Corps. Of course, they didn't know the mercenaries by that name, and none of the four mercs told their clients their real names, but the parents still knew what the four strangers did for a living. Carol and her allies agreed to pay them ten thousand dollars in advance and an additional forty grand after the mission, although they couldn't promise how long it would take to raise the rest of the money.

Fifty thousand dollars was less money than the Hard Corps usually accepted for a mission. Sometimes they received more than a million dollars for an assignment. But the mercenaries didn't have any other missions planned at that time and Carol's group was desperate and needed their help. More than that, they *deserved* it.

Although the Hard Corps were professional mercenaries, they also held to strict principles and a personal code of honor. They never worked just for the money. If they didn't believe in a cause, they wouldn't fight for it. The Hard Corps had never worked for criminals or conducted any missions that were contrary to the interests of the United States or the Free World. They never accepted an assignment that threatened to harm innocent people.

William O'Neal had also been impressed by Carol Henderson. The lady had guts. She had stubbornly continued to oppose the FUL, despite all the setbacks and disappointments, for almost a full year. She had singlehandedly organized the other parents and held the group together with her sense of outrage and desire for justice.

O'Neal couldn't help being curious about the lady. He knew she was divorced and she didn't have much of a social life. Carol was a pleasantly attractive woman, about forty-two years old. Beauty, of course, is in the eye of the beholder, and O'Neal personally liked to "behold" Carol. In fact, she seemed to get better-looking every time he saw her. O'Neal realized that meant he was developing a personal interest in Carol—the kind of interest that could get in the way of his professionalism.

Well, O'Neal figured, as long as he recognized this, he could keep himself from getting careless with the woman. After all, she was their client. O'Neal had never gotten romantically involved with a client. Then again, he'd never *wanted* to get involved with one before.

"What do you think we should do now, Mr. Jones?" Carol inquired, looking up at O'Neal.

"Huh?" The Hard Corps commander replied. He was embarrassed to realize he had been gazing at Carol and paying more attention to her than to the conversation, and he wasn't sure what she meant.

"You're Mr. Jones, remember?" Wentworth whispered to O'Neal. "I'm Smith. Mr. Stevens and Mr. Johnson aren't here right now. Are you going to answer the lady, Jones? Or should I?"

"Knock it off, Smith," O'Neal muttered as he stepped forward. "Well, Ms. Henderson . . . He cleared his throat. "We work for you. What do you want us to do now?"

"We're *all* payin' you, son," Baskin told him. "All us parents are puttin' money into this . . ."

"But *she* hired us," O'Neal replied gruffly. He'd decided he didn't like the way Baskin spoke to Carol earlier so he wasn't very concerned with what the guy thought they should or shouldn't do. "You want us to continue the mission, Ms. Henderson?"

"I didn't know anyone would get killed." Carol frowned. "You told me you wouldn't harm anyone unless it was absolutely necessary for reasons of self-defense."

"I'm sorry, Carol," O'Neal replied. "For what it's worth, we *didn't* harm anyone except in self-defense. At least we didn't shoot anyone unless they came at us. Besides, the gunmen who arrived in the station wagon killed a few of the bikers. These people are vicious."

"You must have suspected that a motorcycle gang would be violent," Roberta Kelton remarked. "Goodness, I would have thought you'd be terrified to confront such people."

"I wasn't talking about the bikers," O'Neal explained. "Those guys were pussycats compared to the triggermen who arrived in the wagon. Odds are they're also working for Glover's cult, and that means your kids are in a lot of danger."

"We already knew that," Baskin complained. "And from what you tell us, my daughter could be down in South America in some kind of whorehouse by now. I say we go to the FBI. This is a job for the Federal government."

"There's no evidence," O'Neal insisted. "The Feds can't do anything and all you'll accomplish by contacting the FBI or any other fed outfit will be to admit you know something about the 'Forest Massacre.' That's what the media's calling all the bodies the cops found at the tavern. So far, everybody thinks another gang of motorcycle outlaws did it. The cult certainly wants the public to believe that and, frankly, it's probably best for us if that opinion continues. My group is gonna have enough trouble just taking on the cult. We don't need any hassles from the cops or the Feds as well."

"I feel obligated to remind all of you that it is imperative that you maintain our secrecy," Wentworth added. The Hard Corps lieutenant was a former intelligence officer and realized the importance of security for an operation—and how easily security could be violated. "If any details about us get beyond this room, we'll be forced to terminate the mission."

"We understand that, Mr. Smith," Carol assured him.

"I sure hope everybody understands," Wentworth stated, turning a critical eye toward Baskin and Roberta.

Wentworth wasn't worried about Carol Henderson. The woman's commitment to rescuing the young people still involved with Glover's cult guaranteed she'd keep her mouth shut. Besides, Carol had agreed to have them meet in her own home in Fresno. At that moment they were gathered together in her neatly kept, modestly furnished living room. She had become too involved with the operation. If the Hard Corps took a fall, Carol would go down with them, and she was smart enough to realize this.

Baskin and Roberta were less reliable, in Wentworth's opinion. Donald Baskin was too impatient. He wanted a quick and easy solution to the problem. Baskin was also understandably worried about his daughter and, possibly, felt guilty about the fact his child had willingly joined the cult. Had he done something wrong as a parent? Was his daughter's plight his fault? Not surprisingly, Baskin was eager to lash out at anyone else—including Carol and the Hard Corps—if it could help ease his own guilt for at least a moment or two.

Roberta Kelton was the opposite of Baskin. She was upset by the idea of taking direct, probably illegal, action against the cult. Two of her children belonged to the cult, a twenty-year-old son and an eighteen-year-old daughter. Her instinct to protect her kids was a powerful motivation for her actions, but Roberta was a law-abiding middle-class housewife, and the concept of hiring mercenaries went against her grain. She was afraid of getting into trouble with the law. She had eventually backed Carol's actions out of love for her children . . . so far, anyway.

"What do you think the chances are that you can accomplish anything against the FUL?" Carol asked O'Neal. "Rescue any of the kids involved with it or expose the criminal activities of Glover and his people?"

"Odds are better now than they were before we started the mission," O'Neal answered. "I know you're all distressed to learn about the drugs and white slavery connection, but bear in mind that this at least gives us a better idea of what Glover has been up to. That means we know more about what sort of contacts the bastard must have with the underworld and what he might do when he learns the Lucifer's Wild Riders are extinct. After all, that's going to put a crimp in his activities. Probably buys us some time. He won't be apt to increase his trafficking in drugs or white slavery until he's sure it's safe to conduct business as usual."

"What about the kids?" Baskin insisted. "Even if you get them free they'll be addicted to dope or turned into . . ." He shuddered. ". . . *prostitutes*."

"Since that was done against their will I'm sure they'll respond to rehabilitation," Wentworth reassured him. "If you think any of these young people are going to come out of this experience unscathed, you're wrong. It'll be tough for them when they get out. But the point is, it's *hopeless* as long as they're still trapped in the cult."

"You know, we thought about getting a deprogrammer," Roberta said. "The problem is, there was so much TV coverage about how they abduct kids back to their parents, that the cults got on to them. Look at Jim Jones. He took everyone down to that country in South America, where deprogrammers couldn't get at 'em."

"Jim Jones was no ordinary cult leader, either," said O'Neal. "And from what I'm learning, neither is Harold Glover. You send in a deprogrammer and Glover will send him back to you in a pine box. But my people won't be so easy to kill. I think we can take the son of a . . ." He caught himself. ". . . creep. I think we can save your kids. For you, Carol, at least you'll know Glover didn't get away with murder. And if you'll recall our terms, if we don't succeed, you don't pay us."

"How do you intend to do it?" Baskin asked. "You plan to kill Glover?"

"We're not planning to do that," O'Neal answered. "But don't be surprised if that happens in the process. These guys seem to like to play rough, and we'll have to be just as tough if we're gonna win. So, Carol. We still workin' for you?"

Carol turned to the other parents. "Donald? Roberta?

You represent the other families involved. What do you say? I think we ought to have a vote."

"I guess there isn't any other way," Roberta answered reluctantly.

"No, there isn't," Baskin announced. "I don't give two hoots 'n' a holler if that Glover fella gets killed, so long as I get my Jenny back."

"Okay, Mr. Jones," Carol said, "you're still working for us. Do what you have to. You don't need to give us any details that we don't need to know."

"That's the way we like to work, ma'am," O'Neal replied with a grim smile.

CHAPTER 3

"PEOPLE HAVE BEEN lying to you all your lives!" Harold Glover stood triumphantly on the platform, facing his congregation. "This society, and every society throughout the world, has been repeatedly poisoned by the lies and corruption of those who would make slaves of you and all the people of the world! Liars who have distorted truth and twisted it, just as they would twist your minds with hatred and prejudice! They've tried their best to keep you ignorant, because it's easy to hate things you don't understand! Isn't it?"

The young people squatting on the grass nodded in unison. Glover smiled and nodded back. His broad grin seemed sincere, his sky-blue eyes were full of the firm conviction of the sanctity of his message, and his rugged, tanned face gave him an honest "working-class" appearance. His straw-colored hair extended to the collar of his shirt. Glover, as always, was wearing white, the color of purity. His shirt, slacks, shoes, and belt were all white. Even the band to his wristwatch was white.

Glover's Australian accent impressed the young Americans. A proper British accent might have seemed too "stuffy" to the American ear. A cockney accent might have been amusing. But the kids were intrigued by the Aussie's accent, which seemed earthy and honest and good-natured.

"And when I'm talking about prejudice I don't just mean blacks and Jews and that sort of thing," Glover explained to his fascinated audience. "Some people are prejudiced toward others because of the color of their skin or religious beliefs or ethnic background, but it goes further than that. You're taught to hate things that are different, but in reality, hatred is only *ignorance!* Ignorance of many things, but primarily . . . ignorance of the Truth!"

The young followers nodded enthusiastically. Their well-scrubbed faces, black-and-white together, looked so much alike to Glover. He had seen so many of them. They smiled and glowed when he spoke. Sometimes he was bored with their obedience and almost wished they'd defy him. But then he'd wax euphoric with the knowledge that he had complete control over them.

Glover smiled before turning serious again. "The Fellowship of Ultimate Living, as you all know, is a *philosophical* society," Glover declared. "Out there they call us a 'cult,' you know. A bunch of weirdos. Just like the Hare Krishnas or even Jim Jones. Funny thing, though! None of you are dressed in robes and bowing and chanting to me. None of you are sitting around drinking Kool-Aid at my bidding. Haven't even made you shave your heads or beg for money at the airports, have I?"

The crowd chuckled in reply. Glover smiled and held up his hands for silence. The crowd immediately obeyed.

"Of *course* we're not a cult," Glover continued, his gaze sweeping over his audience. "And we're *not* concerned with religion or politics here. Not in the general sense of the term. We're concerned with the Truth, with a capital *T*. There is only one Truth, and here, in the Fellowship, it will reveal itself to all of us!"

The crowd applauded warmly, and Glover held up his hands. "Morality is simply a set of rules for living in harmony with other people so all can benefit. That's what you're learning here. How to live in such a manner that you will learn the inner nature of Truth! And *when* you've learned the Truth, *well . . .*" He paused for effect. ". . . there will be nothing else worth learning!"

Glover glanced offstage and noticed Thor Ornjarta standing by the curtain, gesturing for him to end the speech. Glover gave Thor a curt nod and turned once more to his applauding congregation.

"That is the road to life," he pontificated. "It is that simple. Go now, and in whatever form it takes, practice the Truth. Learn the Truth. Live the Truth." The crowd applauded again as Glover bowed and walked back offstage. Some of the young people moaned with disappointment because they wished their leader would continue to speak for at least a while longer. Glover maintained his friendly grin until he was out of view of the crowd.

"Incredible," Glover rasped under his breath. "They're so wrapped-up today I bet I could talk them into eating shit if I told them it was really chocolate fudge. If they didn't . . . *love* me so much, I think I'd give up the whole bloody thing."

"I'm not surprised, Harry," Thor said with a smile. "You surely can weave a spell over people."

"California is a perfect spot for this sort of thing," Glover added. "You know, when I heard that 'anything goes' here I could hardly believe it. But it's true. Come up with a philosophy that has a ring to it . . ."—he looked sharply at Thor—"and people are in your *power*." He chuckled.

"We'll find uses for them, Harry," Thor assured him. "We always have."

Thor Ornjarta was quite familiar with the uses the cult had found for Glover's followers in the past. He'd been Glover's chief enforcer and bodyguard since the FUL had been created two years ago in Australia. The cult hadn't been very successful until Glover had set up this chapter in California. The state had dozens of cults and nobody worried about another one, especially an outfit that claimed to be "philosophical" instead of religious or political.

If anyone had bothered to check into the backgrounds of some of Glover's bodyguards and security personnel, however, they might have become more suspicious of the Aussie's philosophical image. Thor Ornjarta was wanted for murder in his native land of Sweden. The six-foot-six, muscle-bound Swede had actually killed a number of men —and a few women as well. He had a nasty sadistic streak, which had twisted his sex drive into a brutal pattern of beatings, rapes, and occasional murders.

Thor had been smart enough to commit most of his crimes in other European countries, but he'd gotten careless in Stockholm when he had settled an argument in a tavern by bashing in a man's skull with a brass ashtray. Thor had fled to Australia, where he had become a legbreaker for a loan shark in Melbourne. Here he learned to control his violent streak and got his kicks by busting up welchers and slapping around an occasional prostitute.

Like many men with a serial-killer personality, Thor was an intelligent sociopath, and he had soon risen in the underworld ranks to command his own loan-shark operation. Eventually, the big Swede with shoulder-length flame-red hair had come into contact with an ambitious young man named Harold Glover.

"So why did you call me off the stage?" Glover asked Thor as they headed for the cult leader's dressing room. "Something wrong?"

"The guards caught a couple of kids trying to climb the fence last night," Thor answered. "A boy and a girl."

"Had they started to go through conditioning?" Glover's face hardened as he closed the door to his quarters. "If so, what level?"

"They were both in isolation," the Swede answered. "They were being deprived of food, and sleep, too, but they hadn't been given any drugs yet. The girl's a looker. We'd already started working on her a little."

"I'm sure," Glover muttered as he studied his face in a

mirror. "My, but I do look *overpowering* today," he muttered. Turning to Thor, he asked, "Don't you ever get bored with rape?"

"Don't knock it if you haven't tried it," the Swede answered with a cold smile.

"Too much effort for something that lasts a minute or two," Glover replied curtly. "How was she responding to treatment? She still trying to fight you and your mates? Or has she learned to just give up and like it?"

"Still fighting a bit," Thor answered. "Damn near bit off Donally's nose a couple of nights ago. He got a bit mad, naturally, and started punching her up a bit, but we pulled him off before he could mark her up. After all, a girl isn't so pretty after half the bones in her face have been broken."

"I'd just as soon not know about the details, mate," Glover told him as he lit a cigarette—a taboo for the cult leader's image of purity. "How you do what you have to do is your business. How did they break out of isolation?"

"The boy did that," Thor explained. "Their cells were side by side. He managed to work a stone loose from the wall and wriggled through the girl's cell. Schultz entered the girl's cell for a bit of fun. He didn't expect the boy to be there, too. The kids knocked him down and stomped on his face. Cracked an eye socket, but Schultz will probably live. Might lose the eye though."

"Good," the Aussie said with a hard edge in his voice. "That's what the bastard gets for failing to obey orders. None of your people are to go into a cell alone. You can see why I made that rule."

"I didn't do it, Harry," Thor said defensively. "Schultz did. Not me."

"Okay," Glover assured him, aware that Thor's bad temper could explode against anyone, even him if he pushed the Swede too far. "The kids were caught. That's what matters. What kind of shape are they in?"

"Guards worked them over a bit," Thor said. "The boy's arm is broken and his face isn't very nice to look at now.

They went easier on the girl. Broke her nose and knocked loose a tooth or two. Otherwise she's fine."

"Which one is she? The Daniels girl?"

"Cartwright, I think," Thor replied, licking his lips. "A natural blonde, you know."

"Valuable piece of property," Glover remarked. "She'll be worth a lot, that's for certain. Tell your mates to lay off her for a while. Give her a shot of morphine or something to calm her down a bit. The boy is a different matter. Too independent and resourceful to ever make a reliable mule. Even if we turn him into an addict, the little bastard would turn against us eventually. Arrange an accident for him."

"No problem, Harry," Thor assured him.

"Out of state," Glover decided, glancing at a wall map of the western United States. "Make it Oregon this time. Have him crushed by logs or whatever they have in Oregon, so his broken bones aren't a mystery for the police. I want good people to handle this, Thor. You go with them and supervise it yourself if you have the slightest doubt about them. Okay?"

"It'll be taken care of," the Swede promised.

"Good," Glover said with a nod. "I'm a bit worried, you know. What happened to the Lucifer bikers was very odd, Thor. Whoever took them out was very good at that sort of thing. They not only took out most of the gang, but they also killed three of your men."

"I know," Thor said grimly. "When I find out who they are, I'll settle with them. We're working on it now. Do you think that bitch in Fresno has anything to do with this?"

"The Henderson woman?" Glover scoffed. "She's a mere goody-two-shoes counselor for a drug rehabilitation clinic. She wouldn't have the money to hire professional shooters. Even if she did, she wouldn't have the guts to pull a stunt like this. I'll give her credit that she was smart enough to figure out what happened to her daughter, but she wouldn't know how to contact professional hitters."

"I could pay her a visit and make sure," Thor suggested.

"Absolutely not!" Glover replied sharply. "You fool.

Anything happens to that woman and the authorities are going to figure she was right about us after all. Right now she's a grief-stricken mother, looking for someone to blame for her daughter's death. Nobody's paying attention to her and after a while she'll give up."

Thor licked his lips again. "But I saw a picture of her once. She's got nice jugs for someone over forty. Bet she can give good head with a little coaxing."

"That's enough," Glover demanded. Thor was an animal sometimes, and had to be kept in his place. There was a lot more to think about than sex right now. "Forget about Carol Henderson, but try to find out more about the group that slaughtered the bikers. Whoever did it is going to pay, as they say here, to the *max*."

"Very well," Thor agreed. "What about the Cartwright girl?"

"Soften her up for a few days and let her bruises mend," Glover answered. "Then we'll contact our friends and see who offers the best deal. Too bad our contact with the Mexican mob was severed. Try our other sources. They usually trade cocaine for women. The Cartwright girl ought to be worth five or six decagrams. Mixed with enough baking powder or grain sugar and that's almost a kilo of crack. That's worth a small fortune on the streets. Dealers will pay a neat price for that much crack."

Thor looked at Glover with a smile. "I'll be sorry to go back to Australia."

"We've got business to take care of there, too, my friend," Glover reminded him. "Don't worry. You can still have some fun with the merchandise in Australia before we close the deals with our Asian friends and that greasy frog, LeTrec."

Thor's eyes gleamed at the prospect.

CHAPTER 4

THE HARD CORPS' compound and base of operations was located in a dense forest region in the state of Washington. The compound had formerly been the property of a big-time marijuana grower who'd had a booming business in the Northwest until the law caught up with him. He'd sold the land for a relatively low price because he needed money in a hurry to pay for his high-priced lawyer. The Hard Corps eagerly bought the compound, though the pot grower lost his case and went to the state pen on a ten-to-twenty rap. Sometimes you win and sometimes you lose.

The mercenaries had certainly won an ideal location. The compound was positioned near a mountain range, which served as a windbreak against the harsh blizzards in the winter months. The five hundred acres featured lots of trees and a river, which supplied hydroelectric power for the base. There was enough deer and other game to allow for an ample supply of venison, and there were plenty of fish in the river.

The Hard Corps had made a lot of changes in the way the pot growers had run the place. The marijuana plants had already been torn up by the DEA agents and destroyed.

43

The Hard Corps had built their headquarters building on the site. They had also constructed a mess hall and several storage sheds. The six cottages originally built by the grass peddlers had been converted into living quarters for the mercenaries. Each reflected the individual owner's particular tastes.

William O'Neal and James Wentworth had returned to the compound after meeting with Carol Henderson in Fresno. Joe Fanelli and Steve Caine were waiting for them when O'Neal landed the Bell UD-1 helicopter at the Hard Corps' chopper pad.

"You guys just eager to see us or you got some urgent news?" O'Neal inquired as he and Wentworth approached their two teammates.

"Figured we oughta warn you that Old Saintly will be arriving in less than an hour," Fanelli explained. "And I think he's pissed off at us."

"Saintly is *always* pissed off about something," O'Neal remarked. He noticed Fanelli and Caine were dressed in civilian clothing instead of the usual fatigue uniform they generally wore while at the compound. "You going somewhere?"

"Benny the Wizard is supposed to have our papers ready," Caine answered. "Since we might have to move fast on this mission, we thought we'd head to Seattle and try to pick up the forgeries before we have to head back to California."

"That is," Fanelli added, "if we've still got a mission."

"We do," O'Neal confirmed.

"Maybe you ought to talk with Saintly before you decide for sure about that, Captain," Fanelli suggested. "He might have another job lined up for us. Saintly never makes a personal visit here unless there's a good reason, and that reason is usually connected with a job."

"We've got a job, Joe," O'Neal told him. "Saintly will just have to accept that. You want to fly the Bell to Seattle?"

"Beats walkin'," Fanelli said with a grin.

"Okay." O'Neal nodded. "Get the stuff from Benny and get back here pronto. Steve, you make sure Joe doesn't head for his favorite whorehouse."

"If he tries it I'll cut his wang off," Caine said with a solemn nod.

"Jesus," Fanelli moaned. "You guys think I'm irresponsible and go chasing after women like a horny teenager ruled by his hard-on or something?"

"Something like that," Wentworth remarked.

Nobody argued with this.

"Try to get back before sundown," O'Neal told them. "You haven't had much flying time after dark, Joe. I don't want you to try to land the chopper at night unless I'm with you. Okay?"

"Gotcha," Fanelli replied.

Fanelli and Caine climbed into the Bell as O'Neal and Wentworth headed for the heart of the compound. The rotor blades of the chopper whirled violently as Fanelli started up the engine. The helicopter soon rose from the pad and climbed into the noon sky before turning east and heading for Seattle.

"You sure Fanelli's the only one who lets interest in women cloud his judgment?" Wentworth commented as he watched the chopper sail from view.

"This a confession, Jim?" O'Neal inquired.

"I think you know what I'm talking about," Wentworth stated, turning his gaze to fix his eyes on O'Neal's face. "You've got more than a passing interest in Carol Henderson, Bill. You deny it if you want, but we both know it's true. That's the sort of thing that can screw up a mission, and it can affect your ability to make decisions."

"We've all been together for a long time, Jim," O'Neal remarked. "If you want to tell me something, don't fuck around. Tell me directly. You think I've made a mistake about taking on this mission, or not?"

"I'm not sure you would have accepted this job if Carol wasn't our client," Wentworth stated. "It's not the sort of thing the Hard Corps would ordinarily get involved with."

"You make Carol sound like a dragon lady," O'Neal scoffed. "Figure she's cast a spell over me or something?"

"If she was a dragon lady you wouldn't be intrigued by her," Wentworth told him. "She's intelligent, courageous, and she has a lot of heart. That's why she's got you by the balls. She probably doesn't even know it and you sure as hell won't admit it . . ."

"You want out of this one, Jim?" O'Neal demanded. "Figure we ought to scrap the mission and see what Saintly has for us? You think we should tell those parents that they'll just have to get used to the idea their kids are trapped in a goddamn cult that's using them to transport drugs, selling them into white slavery, and killing them? You don't think this mission matters?"

"It matters," the lieutenant assured him. "But it's a high-risk assignment and, realistically, we probably can't hope to do any better than come to a draw with the FUL. The parents aren't paying us enough money to merit the risk. Hell, they may *never* pay us the full fifty grand. What are we going to do if they don't pay us? Sue them? This mission requires that we carry out illegal operations right here in the U.S., and that's not something that makes me feel very comfortable, Bill."

"I don't like to repeat myself," O'Neal declared, "but what the hell do you want to do, Jim?"

"Talk to Saintly before we decide what to do next," Wentworth answered. "Fair enough?"

"Okay," O'Neal agreed. "But first we'll see what Top has for us."

"Top" was John McShayne, a thirty-year Army veteran who'd seen action in Korea and Vietnam. McShayne had worked in several military occupational specialties. He'd been a motor-pool sergeant, a helicopter mechanic, a computer programmer, and a mess sergeant. McShayne had acquired an impressive array of skills and experiences by the time he had left the service.

McShayne didn't want to retire after he left the Army. Instead, he found a different type of Army. McShayne learned that the Hard Corps were recruiting personnel for a mission in Central America. He met with O'Neal and offered his services as a first class NCOIC. McShayne could handle maintenance for automobiles, Jeeps or choppers. He could operate computers, handle bookkeeping, assist in administration and paperwork. He was too valuable to let slip by, and O'Neal knew it.

The Hard Corps were essentially a tiny private army, and every army needs a strong support team to handle clerical, maintenance, payroll, and supply. McShayne was all this and more. He was their top sergeant and as vital to the outfit as any of the four mercenaries on the team.

John McShayne was seated at his desk in the orderly room when O'Neal and Wentworth entered the headshed. The grizzled senior NCO was a big man, built like a beer keg with thick limbs and a heavy square head, emphasized by the close-cropped crew-cut he still wore. McShayne leaned back in his chair and saluted the merc officers with a coffee cup in his fist.

"Welcome back," he greeted. "How's California? I always heard it was full of steers and queers."

"Moo," O'Neal replied. "We ran into a little excitement. I imagine Joe and Steve told you about that."

"Fanelli told me," McShayne said. "Caine doesn't talk much. You know how he is. I'm a little confused about why you blew the shit out of the motorcycle gang, but then Fanelli's never been the best guy to explain things. Anyway, I've been busy with the computers while you fellas were gone. Managed to tap into the data banks of the Department of Immigration and broke that new access code the FBI came up with this week. Got some more stuff on that Fellowship of Ultimate Living."

"So the Feds have been investigating Glover after all," O'Neal mused. "What you got on him, Top?"

"Well," McShayne began, sipping his coffee, "the cult started in Australia and it still has its home base there. Nobody seems to be quite sure where. Somewhere in the outback. You could hide a city in the outback. Anyhow,

Glover's cult is about two years old now. Lot of people have been suspicious about the FUL, but nobody's been able to prove anything so far."

"Doesn't help much," Wentworth remarked.

"Didn't say it would, sir," McShayne replied as he punched the controls of his computer. "Here's what Immigration has on Glover. Want me to read it?"

"If any of it's useful," O'Neal answered.

"Most interesting item is that Immigration has been thinking of having the guy deported," McShayne stated. "Of course, Glover is still an Australian citizen and he commutes to and from his native country a lot. Once again, Immigration can't prove anything, but there've been a lot of complaints about Glover because he always takes a bunch of American kids with him when he leaves California and heads back to Australia. The real kicker is, none of these kids ever seems to come back."

"What's the FBI interested in the cult for?" O'Neal asked.

"Investigating distraught parents' claims of kidnapping," McShayne answered. "But there's no evidence any of the kids were forced to join the FUL or forced to leave the country with Glover. The Feds have also taken an interst in the high mortality rate of so-called former members of the cult."

"I guess if a pattern lasts long enough even the FBI will notice it," O'Neal muttered. "Speaking of Feds, you have any idea what Saintly wants?"

"No," McShayne replied. "But his chopper will be arriving any minute now. Want me to give him permission to land?"

"Not really." The Hard Corps commander sighed. "But I guess we'd better talk to him."

The helicopter arrived five minutes later. The pilot requested permission to land and William O'Neal headed for the helicopter pad to greet their guest. The chopper was a Lynx, piloted by a bush flier who earned some extra money running occasional errands for the Federal government. The sliding door opened and a familiar figure dressed in a gray suit and striped tie emerged.

"Old Saintly" was Joshua St. Laurent, a case officer for the Central Intelligence Agency. St. Laurent was stationed at an office in Canada, where he spent most of his time spying on embassy personnel from the Soviet Union as well as representatives from other embassies—including many who work for governments friendly to the United States. That's how the espionage business works: everybody tries to learn everything possible about everybody else and keep their own secrets in the process.

However, St. Laurent was also an unofficial liaison officer for the Hard Corps—a sort of go-between for the mercenaries and the U.S. government. Uncle Sam never openly hired mercenaries to carry out missions in foreign lands, but occasionally clandestine deals were arranged for such operations to be conducted in secret. Naturally, the CIA got most of the dirty jobs of this kind. If they found a situation that required direct action, the Company never handled this themselves if they could sent in some "experts from the private sector" instead.

Since the Hard Corps were the best mercenaries in the business, the Company had hired them on more than one occasion. Saintly had been their contact and had also arranged a deal with the mercs. The Hard Corps would do Uncle Sam a favor from time to time and, in return for this, the Company would make certain the IRS didn't pry into the mercs' financial affairs. The CIA would also keep the BATF off their ass about certain weapons and explosives kept at the compound. The Feds would also take care of other agencies that might cause problems for the Hard Corps, including the FCC, Housing Commissions, and even the United States Army itself, since Steve Caine was still listed as an MIA and could, by distorting some facts, be tried as a deserter.

Naturally, these benefits could be turned into threats if the Hard Corps failed to oblige. O'Neal and his men were aware of this, but the deal still offered more advantages than disadvantages. St. Laurent passed on information about potential operations and occasionally warned the mercs about certain job offers that were undesirable. The hint of blackmail involved with the deal wasn't so bad because the mercenaries could always abandon the compound and set up elsewhere if the Feds decided to make life uncomfortable. However, so far the arrangement had worked out for all involved.

St. Laurent had no illusions about his relationship with the Hard Corps. The CIA man didn't control the mercenaries and he knew they wouldn't respond well if he pushed them. The mercs were patriots and they'd never do anything that would threaten national security, but they wouldn't blindly follow orders just because some Fed sneaky-pete type told them to do it. They were fiercely independent and they weren't very fond of government agencies or following anybody's rules and regulations.

"Hello, O'Neal," St. Laurent chimed. "You guys have fun in California?"

"What makes you think we were in California?" the Hard Corps boss replied as they strolled from the helipad.

"They found eighteen bodies at a little roadside bar," the CIA man began. "Several had been shot to death with Uzi submachine guns and M-16 rifles. A couple were shot with arrows dipped in curare, I believe. One guy had been cut and stabbed by a weapon believed to be a sword. That sounds an awful lot like a certain band of crazy mercenaries I know have been busy in the Sunshine State."

"Florida is the Sunshine State," O'Neal commented. "California is the land of steers and queers. What the hell do you want, Saintly?"

"Do you have to call me that?" St. Laurent sighed.

"The name suites you," O'Neal replied. "Patron saint of national security. What's your interest in what goes on in California? CIA is only supposed to operate outside the United States. Mind you, I'm not saying we were in California or that we know anything about what happened."

"And you aren't interested in Harold Glover or the Fellowship of Ultimate Living?" Saintly inquired. "In that case, I'll tell my chopper jockey to fly me back across the border..."

"Okay," the Hard Corps commander announced. "We did it. Happy now? So tell me why the CIA is interested in Glover and his goddamn cult."

"Glover has established an international organization," St. Laurent began. "Not just in the United States and Australia. He has contacts in Central and South America."

"Tell me something I don't know," O'Neal said with a shrug.

"Do you know about Thailand? Japan? Vietnam?" St. Laurent inquired, obviously pleased by the surprise in O'Neal's expression.

"No," the merc leader admitted. "But I sure hope you'll enlighten me about this."

"Tell you what I can," Saintly answered. "It seems Glover has contacts with the Golden Triangle dope dealers in Southeast Asia. His people are being used as mules to transport heroin out of Thailand, Laos, and Vietnam. A couple of brainwashed American kids got caught in Bangkok and wound up serving time in Thailand for smuggling. We also think he's been selling girls to the markets in Southeast Asia, Japan, maybe even India. The guy's got quite a setup. DEA and drug enforcement in a dozen other countries have been trying to nail that bastard for some time."

"Is he managing this from his base in the outback?" O'Neal said with a frown. "Of course! Australia is in the goddamn Pacific. I wouldn't be surprised if he's dealing with gangsters in the Philippines as well."

"O'Neal," Saintly insisted, "you'd better listen to me. The CIA has gotten involved because Glover is doing business with connections in 'Nam and Laos. He might decide to move into the espionage business. He's already got a better clandestine setup than a lot of Third World countries have been able to manage. Leave him alone, O'Neal. Let us handle him."

"When the hell are you government hotshots going to get around to taking care of him, Saintly?" O'Neal demanded.

"How do I know?" the CIA operative replied with a shrug. "Look, Bill. I'm one tiny little cog in Uncle Sam's great big intelligence machine. They don't tell me a hell of a lot and the only reason they told me this much is because my superiors at Langley want you guys to back off. What you did stirred up a lot of heat on us. The FBI figures we did that number on those motorcycle hoods. The NSA probably figures we did it, too. You do know what the NSA is?"

"The National Security Agency," O'Neal said with a nod. "It's actually the largest intelligence network in the United States government. Bigger than the CIA or the FBI. Also has the lowest profile among you spy outfits. Most Americans are only vaguely aware it even exists."

"That's right," Saintly confirmed. "And the NSA spies on everybody. They're the only American intel outfit authorized to conduct operations here in the U.S. and abroad. They spy on CIA and FBI operations, too. They're going to be checking up on us more now that you've pulled that stunt in California."

"Come on," O'Neal snorted. "You guys exaggerate stuff like this. You're trying to find excuses to convince us to lay off the FUL cult. You guys are so damn paranoid about the 'other side' finding out *anything* you know that you spend too much time keeping secrets from everybody— even the people on your own side—to take any action. This situation requires action and it requires it damn soon. Harold Glover is even worse than I thought he was. We can't let him go on with business as usual, Saintly."

"And we all want to stop him—" Saintly began lamely.

"When?" O'Neal demanded, rolling his eyes toward the sky. "There are almost four hundred young people who've joined his cult in the last year and a half, Saintly. Some of them are already dead. Some others are probably lost forever. The only hope the rest of them have is if Glover's outfit is brought to an end once and for all. That'll free the kids inside the cult itself and, providing that jerk kept some sort of records about the kids he's sold into slavery, we might be able to find a lot of the missing ones as well."

"You're the most stubborn son of a bitch I've ever met, O'Neal," Saintly said with exasperation. "What do you think you're gonna do? Attack the California branch of the FUL and then charge over to Australia to finish off the home base of the cult?"

"Something like that," O'Neal admitted.

"Oh, God," Saintly moaned. "Okay. You can find the California branch easy enough, that's no state secret."

"Thank God *something* isn't," O'Neal muttered.

"But what about the cult base in the Australian outback?" Saintly demanded. "You don't have any idea where it is."

"I bet there are people in the CIA and NSA who know," the Hard Corps leader remarked.

"I'm sure there are," St. Laurent agreed. "But they aren't going to tell you the location and they aren't going to tell me because I don't have a need to know. If I get too curious about it, they'll figure out why. Don't be surprised if the Company tries to stop you on this one, O'Neal. There's not a damn thing I can do about it."

"This is nuts," O'Neal groaned. "I thought we were more or less on the same side. What's the CIA want to protect Glover for? That's what they'll be doing if they stop us!"

"They don't look at it that way," Saintly explained. "The Company figures you're a bull in a china shop, O'Neal. They figure you'll ruin everything for them."

"They can go fuck themselves for all I care," O'Neal shot back. "The Company can mentally masturbate all it wants to. My team has a mission and you haven't said anything to make me change my mind about that, Saintly."

"I was afraid you'd say that," the CIA man muttered, shaking his head. "Well, I'll see if I can find any intel that can help you guys. No promises, except I'll give you my word that our conversation will remain confidential."

"I appreciate that," O'Neal assured him. He meant it. Saintly was a desk jockey, but it still took guts to risk his job for the sake of the Hard Corps. Especially since the Company would never let him leave without dogging his ass for the rest of his life. Saintly knew too much to let him run around without any watchdogs.

"One other thing I feel I should mention," Saintly added. "If you manage to get to Glover's Australian base, there's pretty good evidence that his contacts in the Pacific include a Triad syndicate connected with the Golden Triangle. You know about the Triad?"

"Not much," O'Neal admitted. "Chinese criminal society sort of like the old tong outfits. Wentworth is interested in stuff like that. He probably knows a lot more about it than I do."

"I've known some agents who were stationed in Singapore and Bangkok," Saintly remarked. "They said they were more scared of the Triad than they were of enemy agents. Triad makes the Vietcong look like old ladies. Try to avoid them. If you wind up on a Triad death list, I don't think even *your* considerable abilities will be much help."

"Thanks for the warning," O'Neal assured him.

"Sure," St. Laurent replied as he turned to head back to the helicopter. "You know, you guys may have really bitten off a lot more than you can chew this time. In fact, you might be the ones to get eaten on this mission. When it's over, if you're still alive, I'm going to be very curious to know if you figure it was worth it."

CHAPTER 5

BENJAMIN WALLGREEN WAS known to special customers as "Benny the Wizard." Wallgreen operated a small office-supplies and copying service business on Second Street. Officially, he barely made enough money to get by. However, he made a much larger profit with his unofficial business arrangements, which he kept secret from the IRS.

Benny the Wizard was the best forger in Seattle, perhaps the best on the entire West Coast. His work was so good even experts had difficulty recognizing a forgery by the Wizard. Benny's unique skills were in great demand among people who needed high-quality forgeries. Not everyone could afford the Wizard's services, but those who could meet his price were always pleased with his product.

The Hard Corps had been among Benny's regular customers ever since they'd set up the compound in Washington state. The mercenaries often needed new identities for a mission and frequently came to the Wizard to print up passports, visas, driver's licenses, phony social security cards, forged birth certificates, and other documents.

The small, gnomelike printer had closed his shop that day, but he waited for the Hard Corps to arrive for their special order. Joe Fanelli and Steve Caine entered an alley and knocked on the back door to the print shop. Benny opened it and hastily ushered his visitors inside. He bolted the door after they entered.

"Something wrong, Benny?" Fanelli inquired. The Wizard was always nervous, but today he seemed shakier than usual.

"I just want to handle business quickly today," Benny said with an unconvincing grin that would have looked more natural on a jack-o'-lantern. "I'm going on a vacation right after we wrap up business. I'll be out of town for a couple of months."

"A vacation for reasons of health?" Steve Caine guessed.

"Exactly," Benny admitted. "And my health won't be very good if I stay in Seattle for the next few days. Oh, you did bring the money?"

"Yeah," Fanelli said with a nod. "Fifteen hundred bucks."

"And that is cash?" Benny asked, peering over the rims of the magnifier-eyeglasses perched low on his nose.

"What did you expect?" Fanelli replied. "Seashells and glass beads? Come on, Wiz. We've always been straight-shooters with you. You always deal in cash, so that's what we pay you."

"Sorry, sorry," Benny said, scurrying across the room to a metal filing cabinet. "I'm just rather eager to have as much ready cash as possible for my vacation."

"Things can get pretty expensive when you're on the run," Caine said with a shrug. "Give us our goods and we'll be on our way, Benny."

"You in trouble with the law, or somethin' worse?" Fanelli inquired as the Wizard unlocked his cabinet and slid a drawer open. "Anything we can do to help?"

"Let's not pry into the man's personal problems," Caine told his partner. "We're not going to do anything for him except pay him for his merchandise."

"Hell, Steve," Fanelli complained. "I just asked—"

"Believe me," Benny replied. "You don't want to know. *I* don't want you to know."

The back room of the shop was a cluttered storage area with cabinet shelves of office supplies, stacks of boxes containing various types of paper and sheets of cardboard, and some special copying machines. The Wizard also had a special metal-punch press and a professional photographer's setup with a darkroom in the back.

"Here are the passports and special visas for Australia," Benny announced, handing the booklets to the mercenaries. "You fellas sure travel a lot."

"Goods and services," Caine remarked as he inspected two of the passports. One had his picture on it although the name under the faded photo was Edward Stevens. The other passport was printed up for "George M. Jones," which was William O'Neal's new identity.

"I've also got your driver's licenses, social security cards, and military dog tags ready," Benny declared. "I notice you fellows always have dog tags made up to suit your new identities."

"We can change our names and social security numbers," Fanelli explained, "but not our blood types. If we get wounded, we want to make sure we get the right blood for transfusions."

"You fellas get wounded very often?" Benny asked.

"It's been known to happen," Caine said with a shrug.

"I don't think I want to know any details about what you fellas do," the shriveled little forger said, raising his quivering hands as if to fend off invisible attackers. "Look over the merchandise. Let me know if you've any complaints. Afraid I don't have time to make any major changes, but I can alter dates, names, numbers."

"Everything looks fine," Caine assured him, examining the other documents. "Looks like you've earned your pay once more, Benny."

"Fine," the Wizard said with a nod. "Now, let's—"

The unexpected crash from the front of the shop startled the three men. Benny gasped and retreated toward the back door. It also burst open, the lock broken by a well-placed kick. Joe Fanelli reached under his jacket for the snub-nosed .357 Magnum, and Steve Caine's hand moved toward the handle of the survival knife at the small of his back.

"Freeze, Benny," a voice growled, accompanied by the click of a safety catch pressed forward. "Or I'll blow your fuckin' head off!"

Two men had entered through the rear door. A heavyset guy dressed in a dirty raincoat pointed a sawed-off shotgun at Benny's face. The terrified printer stared into the twin barrels of the invader's weapon. His eyes swelled with terror as if gazing into two tunnels of doom.

The other invader was smaller than his partner, but held another cut-down shotgun. He pointed his double-barreled cannon at Fanelli and Caine. The mercs realized even if they could manage to shoot or stab the gunman, the twitch of a trigger finger by the dying man would be enough to fire the shotgun. A single burst of buckshot could easily blast both mercenaries into oblivion.

"Take it easy," Caine urged, raising his empty hands to shoulder level. "Nobody needs to get hurt."

"Somebody is *gonna* get hurt," the larger man growled as he suddenly swooped his arms in a short arch and drove the abbreviated buttstock of his shotgun into Benny's stomach.

The forger doubled up and fell to his knees, vomiting on the floor near the big goon's jackboots. The brute cursed when some puke splattered his pant cuff. He swung a vicious kick to the side of Benny's head and sent the little man sprawling across the floor.

"Hey, that's not necessary," Fanelli remarked, holding both hands at the back of his head. "You wanna kill him?"

"That's right," the smaller gunman confirmed with a wide grin across his lean, unshaven face. "We *are* gonna kill him. Maybe we'll kill you shitheads, too, if you give us any crap."

"We don't want to give you any crap," Caine said in a calm, even tone. "This isn't any of our business—"

"Shut up!" the gunman ordered, his eyes wide and wild. It wouldn't take much to convince him to pull the trigger.

"Tim? Russell?" a voice barked from the front room. "You guys catch that bastard?"

"We got 'im, Leon!" the smaller hood replied.

A well-muscled black man appeared at the entrance of the supply section. He held a .38-caliber revolver in his fist as he shifted his unblinking gaze from Caine and Fanelli to the dazed forger sprawled on the floor. He frowned as he stared at the two mercs.

"Who are they?" Leon asked, putting the .38 in the waistband of his trousers. He wore Levi's, a fishnet undershirt, and a brown leather jacket. Two white feathers jutted from a red headband to cover his left ear.

"Just a couple of Benny's customers, Leon," the crazy little gunman replied.

"That's great, Tim," the black guy muttered. "They know our names now. Seen our faces. Fuckin' pity. Dudes are probably just like us, only they ain't so lucky."

"Yeah," Tim sneered. "Looks like we'll have to kill them, too. Poor dumb sons of bitches."

"Hell," Fanelli remarked, still holding his hands at the back of his head, "we ain't gonna squeal on you fellas. We'd get ourselves in trouble with the law, too. Ain't no skin off my ass what happens to Benny now."

"Help me," Benjamin Wallgreen groaned as he raised his head and stared up at Fanelli and Caine. Blood oozed from split skin above his temple. "Please . . ."

"Sorry, Benny," Caine told him. "You're on your own now."

"Don't you go beggin' for these dudes to help you," Leon told the forger. "You oughta be beggin' them to forgive you 'cause we're gonna have to kill them because of you."

"What's your beef with Benny?" Fanelli asked.

"We stole somethin' for him," Leon answered. "An ex-

pensive piece of merchandise. A kinda laser light-intensity
device used to make holograms on photographic film.
Don't ask me how it works. I just stole the damn thing."

"What the hell are you doing messing with lasers and
holograms, Benny?" Fanelli began. "Oh, wait a minute.
Those are three-dimensional pictures, right? The sort of
thing they're using on credit cards and stuff these days."

"You have to be able to make holograms now to forge
credit cards," Benny muttered. "That's why almost nobody
does it anymore . . ."

"But Benny planned to do it," Leon snorted. "Gonna be
a big man. Weren't you, Benny? But you needed a laser
setup to do it. A setup worth half a million bucks. That's
how much the asshole paid us for the lasers."

"So what's the problem?" Fanelli asked with a shrug,
still keeping his hands on the back of his skull. Then it hit
him. "Shit, Benny, don't tell me you paid these guys with
counterfeit money."

"Excellent counterfeits," the Wizard replied lamely as
he sat with his back to a wall. "I didn't think they'd realize
what happened for a while—"

"Shut up, motherfucker!" Tim snarled. "You cheated us
and now you're gonna pay."

"Yeah," the big man, Russell, growled as he broke open
his shotgun and dumped the shells on the floor. "And I'm
gonna be the one to collect."

He reached inside his raincoat and removed a large claw
hammer with a steel head. Russell smiled as he put the
shotgun on the floor and stepped forward. Leon reached
into his hip pocket and pulled a switchblade. He pressed
the button and a six-inch blade snapped into place. The
black man approached silently.

"Gotta do this quiet," Leon explained. "I'm really sorry
about this, but we gotta kill you two guys, too. Make it
easy on yourselves, okay? Get down on your knees with
your backs turned and close your eyes. Russ will hit you
hard enough to make sure he kills you with one blow each.
Nice and quick. Best we can do under the circumstances."

"You guys are all heart," Caine commented dryly. "What if we decide to put up a struggle?"

"Fuck you!" Tim snarled as he stepped forward and swung a butt stroke at Caine's face.

The tall bearded mercenary weaved away from the walnut stock of the shotgun. It whirled past his face, missing his nose by less than an inch. His left hand quickly grabbed the frame of the cut-down shotgun before Tim could correct the aim. Caine held the gun away from himself and drew the survival knife from his belt.

Caine plunged the six-inch blade under the gunman's ribs. Tim screamed as blood bubbled into his throat. Caine turned sharply to wrench the shotgun from his opponent's grasp and yank the knife blade free. He lashed the heavy barrels of the scatter gun across Tim's face to knock the would-be assassin to the floor. Unconscious, Tim wasn't even aware that he was bleeding to death.

Russell rushed forward. Fanelli's arms swung from his head to reveal the snub-nosed Magnum in his fist. The barrel pointed directly at Russell's face. The big man stopped abruptly and dropped his hammer. He raised his hands, still staring into the muzzle of Fanelli's .357 revolver.

"Cute trick, huh?" Fanelli remarked, pistol pointed at the horrified man's face. "Wanna see another one?"

He suddenly kicked Russell between the legs. The big man gasped and started to fold up from the terrible pain in his crotch. Fanelli quickly hooked his left fist to the goon's jaw and punched the butt of his Magnum into the point of Russell's chin.

The brute half-turned and fell to all fours. He uttered a moaning, choking sound. Fanelli kicked him in the ribs and hammered the revolver butt behind Russell's ear. The big guy fell on his face in a senseless lump. Fanelli stomped a boot heel between his opponent's shoulder blades to make certain Russell wasn't faking. He needn't have bothered.

Leon lunged at Caine, switchblade striking like the head

of a cobra. Caine dodged the thrust and parried the black man's blade with his survival knife. The switchblade hit the sawtooth back of Caine's blade. Caine adroitly twisted his wrist and drew the cutting edge of his knife across his opponent's wrist. Leon howled in agony as the switchblade fell from his fingers.

Caine's left hand grabbed Leon's neck, clawed fingers gripping into flesh like the talons of a bird of prey. Leon tried to draw the .38 from his belt, but Caine's knife was quicker. The mercenary drove the survival blade deep into his opponent's chest. Sharp steel punctured the man's heart. Caine gripped Leon's throat to muffle the dying man's scream.

Steve Caine felt his opponent's strength fade as Leon rapidly died. The merc held the man's throat and dug his thumbs into the windpipe to hasten Leon's death. The thug's pain was minimal and he was dead within seconds. Caine pried the knife from Leon's lifeless flesh. The sawtooth blade caught on the sternal bone, but Caine worked the knife a bit and pulled it free.

"Oh, my God," Benny the Wizard gasped in astonishment.

"Here's your money," Caine told him, calmly handing the forger a fistful of bills. "Might hire somebody to help you clean up this mess. We gotta be going."

"Yes," Benny said, nodding silently. "Thank you. You . . . saved my life. I won't forget that."

"Saved ourselves, too," Caine reminded him. "Try to stay out of trouble in the future, Wizard. We hope to do business with you again."

"And do yourself a favor, Ben," Fanelli added. "If you hire somebody to help you, pay them with *real* money next time."

CHAPTER 6

THE MUNROE THEATER was located in Elk Grove, just outside of Sacramento. The theater had once been a popular entertainment spot where Hollywood stars attended movie premieres in the Sacramento area. But nowadays, although Sacramento remained the capital of California, emphasis on state activities, business, and entertainment was centered in Los Angeles and the other cities to the south. So the film stars no longer wasted their time coming to the Munroe Theater because the publicity wasn't worth the effort. The theater became a porno house in the early sixties and then featured classic oldies in the seventies. By 1980, the Munroe Theater was virtually bankrupt. The popularity of videocassettes hurt the theater business in general and forced many smaller theaters to shut down entirely. The Munroe Theater was doomed to this fate as well.

However, the new owners of the theater received financial assistance from entrepreneurs who regarded the forty-three-year-old building as a semihistoric relic, which could be preserved by renting it to amateur acting groups for the production of plays. The Munroe Theater was also used by businessmen to present lectures on new products and sales proposals. Real estate seminars were conducted at the theater. Even a few bachelor parties were held there, where a wide screen made viewing stag films more entertaining than seeing them in somebody's living room.

The Fellowship of Ultimate Living had rented the Munroe Theater for a rally. The California branch of the cult was located to the north of Sacramento, but the base was remote and too far from any major city to recruit new members without holding rallies elsewhere. These were usually conducted in Los Angeles, San Francisco, or sometimes in San Diego. Sacramento was convenient although it didn't attract the crowds found in the larger cities.

The Hard Corps had no trouble learning about the rally. The FUL had advertised in several newspapers and a few national magazines weeks in advance. The mercs arrived in Sacramento the day before the event. They drove to the theater and parked a rented Toyota van in front of the building. The streets were quiet and virtually deserted at midnight.

"There might be a night watchman or an alarm system," O'Neal reminded the others. "Be careful."

"If we encounter any problems we'll contact you by walkie-talkie," Wentworth promised as he slipped on a pair of black felt gloves. He glanced at the old movie house. "Rather doubt that anybody's bothered with paying for much security for this place."

"Don't take anything for granted," O'Neal insisted. He stared at the headlights of an approaching automobile; the car passed them without slowing down.

"It's gonna be kind of borin' hanging around inside that place for more than twelve hours," Fanelli remarked, shaking his head as if the idea was too dreadful to contemplate.

"You won't be in there with us," Caine remarked as he slid a .45 Colt into a shoulder holster inside his black windbreaker. "All you have to do is pick the lock for us."

"No sweat." Fanelli smiled. "I was the best lock picker in my neighborhood back in Jersey. My friends counted on me whenever we wanted to borrow a car."

"Can we listen to tales about your misspent youth at another time?" Wentworth muttered as he clipped the two-way radio to his belt.

"Lucky thing I grew up where I did and learned on the streets instead of at West Point," Fanelli replied. "They didn't teach you how to pick locks at that fancy-ass academy, did they?"

"Maybe one day you'll teach a course on the subject," Wentworth said dryly. "Of course, you'll have to get a teacher's certificate, but that shouldn't be too difficult as long as Benny the Wizard is still in business."

"If Benny keeps messing around with characters like those three we encountered at his store, he won't be doing anything but feeding fish at the bottom of Puget Sound," Caine commented. "You ready, Lieutenant?"

"Yeah," Wentworth confirmed as he tucked a compact folding umbrella under his arm. "Let's go."

Wentworth, Caine, and Fanelli emerged from the van and hurried to a dark alley next to the theater. O'Neal stepped from the Toyota and walked to the front of the vehicle. The Hard Corps commander opened the hood and pretended to examine the engine while the other three disappeared into the shadows.

"There she is," Fanelli whispered as he located a side door to the theater. "Looks like a piece of cake. Sure hope so. Be nice to have something easy for a change."

"Bitch, bitch, bitch," Caine said softly.

Fanelli took a key ring from his pocket and switched on a small penlight. He examined the door at the hinges and knob. He found no trace of wires to a burglar alarm, but there could be a subtle setup he couldn't detect from the outside. *You take your chances,* Fanelli thought fatalistically.

He knelt by the doorknob and inserted a thin hacksaw blade into the keyhole. Fanelli probed with the blade and selected a thin metal pick from the keyring. He slipped the probe into the keyhole and gingerly turned both instruments. A soft click announced his success.

"Got it," Fanelli remarked as he turned the knob. The door moved slightly, but refused to open. "Almost."

"Piece of cake, huh?" Wentworth asked sarcastically.

"Hold on," Fanelli urged. "I know what it is. There's a latch bolt on the inside. Gimme a couple seconds, okay?"

Fanelli removed a wire coat hanger from the small of his back. He stretched out the wire to full length and bent it into a U shape. He slowly slid the wire through the crack of the door above the knob. Fanelli's hands moved up and down as he worked the ends of the wire and probed with the portion inside the door.

"I got it now," he declared, and pulled the wire with both hands. "Open Sesame Street, Jack."

He nudged the door with an elbow. It creaked open. Fanelli stood and extended a hand toward the open door in an exaggerated gesture. Wentworth and Caine tapped fingertips against palms in a simulated version of applause. Fanelli bowed in response.

"There may be hope for you yet," Wentworth admitted as he stepped inside the building. "Although I still have my doubts."

"Love you, too, Lieutenant," Fanelli replied with a grin.

Caine followed Wentworth across the threshold and closed the door. Fanelli heard the latch bolt slide into place. He knelt by the doorknob and used the lock picks to relock the door. Fanelli pocketed his burglar tools and headed for the mouth of the alley.

He sucked air through clenched teeth when he saw the police patrol car parked next to the Toyota van. O'Neal was talking to a uniformed cop at the driver's side of the prowl car. Fanelli was relieved that the cops hadn't gotten out of their vehicle. That meant they weren't too suspicious about the Toyota. The revolving lights on the top of the fuzzmobile weren't on, another sign that the police figured O'Neal was a genuine driver in distress.

"Hi, officers," Fanelli announced as he stepped from the alley, aware his voice sounded nervous. He played his role to suit the mood. "I admit I was gonna piss in the alley, but

I really didn't. Honest. When I heard you drive up, I suddenly felt like I could wait until I got home."

"Go ahead and take a leak, fella," the cop behind the steering wheel invited. "So long as you don't do it in the street."

"Thanks," Fanelli replied. Under the circumstances, he welcomed the opportunity to relieve himself.

"Make it quick, Tom," O'Neal urged. "I think I got the engine fixed. Like to get home before your sister wants my head on a platter."

"Brother-in-law, huh?" the cop inquired.

"Yeah," O'Neal answered with a groan. "Dumb ass lost his job in Detroit and he came out here lookin' for one. My wife won't get off my back until I get the bum some kind of job. Heard that they needed a bartender over at the Wooden Nail. Turned out they hired somebody earlier tonight. Just my luck. Between you and me, I don't think he's too eager to find a job. Know what I mean?"

"Stayin' at your place, huh?" The cop shook his head. "Goddamn in-laws are a pain in the ass. My wife's got a brother like that, too. Oughta arrest him for freeloading."

"Wanna collar Tom?" O'Neal asked with a grin.

"Sorry, pal," the cop laughed. "Next time let him piss in the street."

"I'll remember that," O'Neal said with a nod. "Better see if I fixed this hunk of junk."

He climbed into the Toyota and started the engine. Fanelli emerged from the alley and raised his arms in exaggerated surprise at the roar of the Toyota engine. He put down the hood and headed for the passenger side. O'Neal and Fanelli waved good-bye to the police as the cop car headed down the street.

"Jesus," O'Neal said as he eagerly lit a cigarette. "I was afraid everything was gonna fuck up for us when those guys showed up. Nice performance, Joe."

"You weren't so bad yourself, Captain," Fanelli replied, reaching for his own cigarettes. "Didn't have any trouble getting Wentworth and Steve inside. They must be okay. If they'd tripped an alarm or seen a watchman, we'd probably know it by now."

"Yeah," O'Neal agreed, putting the van in drive to pull away from the curb. "Let's go back to the hotel and take turns sleeping. We're gonna need all the rest we can get . . ."

"Desert Fox, this is Desert Rat," Wentworth's voice announced from a walkie-talkie on the seat next to O'Neal. "Do you read me, Desert Fox? Over."

"Hello, Desert Rat," O'Neal replied into the radio unit. "Read you loud and clear. Everything okay for you? Over."

"So far everything is nice and quiet," Wentworth assured him. "We're going to look for a good place to spend the night. Suggest you do likewise. Over."

"Agreed, Desert Rat," O'Neal said. "We'll keep our ears up in case you need to contact us. Understand? Over."

"Affirmative," Wentworth replied. "Don't call us. We'll call you. Over and out."

"Sure hope they'll be okay," Fanelli remarked, crushing out a cigarette in the car ashtray.

"They'll be careful," O'Neal said, trying to reassure himself as well as Fanelli. "They know what to do. Nobody's going to be in much danger until the rally starts."

Wentworth and Caine had been placed inside the theater before the rally in order to have time to inspect the building, become familiar with the theater, and learn all the strategic points and exits in an emergency. They would also be in an ideal position to assist O'Neal and Fanelli when the Hard Corps carried out the next phase of their operation. At least, that was the theory behind their strategy.

When the FUL rally began at two o'clock in the afternoon, the Hard Corps would find out how well their theory worked in reality.

CHAPTER 7

JAMES WENTWORTH AND Steve Caine were crowded under the stairs to the basement of the Munroe Theater. They heard the footfalls of men's feet thud against the steps. The mercs saw the polished black oxfords and cuffs of expensive Italian suit trousers as they peered between the wooden risers. Two men descended the stairs. They were young and athletic, well dressed and clean-cut, with short hair and shaven faces. One man was black and the other white, but otherwise they were virtually identical.

"Look at that furnace," the black guy remarked. "Haven't seen an old coal one like that since I was a kid back in Cleveland. Wonder if it still works."

"We sure don't need it today," the white man replied. He glanced about the basement, sweeping the beam of a flashlight around the dark room. "Sure isn't much else down here. No way for anybody to get in except by these stairs."

"Yeah," the black man agreed. "They even bricked up the chute for the coal. Guess the furnace doesn't work after all."

"Guess not," the white guy agreed. "Fuck it. Let's fin-

ish checkin' this joint out so the Aussie can get his goddamn show started."

"I hate these stupid rallies," the other man muttered as
they mounted the stairs. "Who the fuck does Glover think
he is? The goddamn President or somethin'?"

"Maybe he thinks he's the Pope," the guy's partner
chuckled as the pair reached the head of the stairs. "Somebody tried to kill him too, you know. Guess Glover figures
he can't be too careful."

"Paranoid shithead," the black dude remarked as he shut
the door.

Wentworth and Caine waited, to be certain no one else
was going to inspect the basement. They were crammed
together under the stairs, breathing silently through open
mouths. Both men still held silencer-equipped pistols in
their fists. A full minute passed before either spoke.

"We have to quit meeting like this," Caine whispered.

"I hope so," Wentworth muttered as he slid out from
under the stairs. The sound of hundreds of footsteps thun-
dered over the basement ceiling. The murmur of dozens of
voices accompanied the footfalls. "Sounds like the rally's
starting."

"They're behind schedule," Caine remarked, checking
the luminous dial of his wristwatch. "But it sounds like a
full house."

"Wonderful," Wentworth said with disgust. "The Australian Pied Piper of Scuzz is still packing them in."

He raised the antenna to his walkie-talkie and switched
on the radio to call "Desert Fox." O'Neal's voice replied.

"Glover's security people searched the building, but
failed to find us," Wentworth said into the walkie-talkie.
"They didn't seem to check very carefully. Don't appear to
suspect anything. Over."

"Good," O'Neal's voice replied. "We're in position outside. We've been watching the crowd going in. Mister Ma-
nipulation himself arrived in a big white limo,
accompanied by half a dozen guys who looked like Central
Casting extras for a Mafia movie."

"We saw two of them," Wentworth confirmed. "Stand by and we'll let you know when we're ready to move. Over."

"Affirmative," O'Neal assured him. "The big guy with long red hair went inside with Glover. The one who looks like a professional wrestler in an Italian suit. You remember him?"

"Yes," Wentworth answered. "We noticed him when we had the retreat under surveillance. Pretty sure he's Glover's chief bodyguard. We'll keep an eye out for that one. He must be something special. Over."

"Don't take any chances with *any* of those jokers," O'Neal insisted. "But remember, we don't want any bloodshed unless there's absolutely no way to avoid it. Understand? Over."

"Understood," Wentworth assured him. "We'll contact you as soon as we're ready to welcome you in."

Wentworth and Caine dusted each other off and prepared to head upstairs. Both men donned wide-brim rain hats and glasses with clear lenses. Wentworth pasted a thick, bushy mustache to his upper lip with some spirit gum and Caine laced his beard with some gray powder to create the illusion that he might be five or six years older than his thirty-six years.

Both men had worn black felt gloves since they had entered the theater more than fourteen hours earlier. They had even kept the gloves on as they ate sandwiches and drank coffee from their thermos, which remained hidden under the stairs.

They heard the applause of the crowd overhead. Harold Glover's voice echoed within the auditorium and reached the basement. His pleasant tone and earthy Australian accent didn't sound the least bit sinister. No doubt that was why he'd been such a successful cult leader. It was easy to understand why so many people had been attracted to the Fellowship of Ultimate Living. Glover seemed honest, charming, and full of goodwill. The guy would have seemed more natural doing commercials for tourism than putting on this front for a white-slave ring.

Wentworth and Caine completed their simple disguises and climbed the stairs. They concealed their .45 Colt pistols in specially designed shoulder holsters, which would accommodate the additional bulk of the nine-inch silencers attached to the threaded barrels of the pistols. Wentworth also carried his umbrella and the walkie-talkie. Caine's trusty survival knife was in its sheath at the small of his back.

The Hard Corps lieutenant reached the top of the stairs first. He listened by the door before he turned the knob. Wentworth opened it just a crack to peer into the narrow hallway beyond. He saw the same two security strongmen who had formerly been seen in the basement. The pair were standing in the corridor, quietly talking. The black hood lit a cigarette.

Wentworth turned to Caine and held up two fingers. The bearded merc nodded in response and drew his survival knife. He unscrewed the butt end of the handle to remove the wire saw from the hollow hilt. Caine took two metal rings from the butt-cap and attached one to each end of the saw. He removed two short oak sticks from his pocket, each only four inches long, and slid them through the rings.

Certain Caine was ready, Wentworth eased the door open and stepped into the hall. He staggered forward, holding the umbrella in both hands. Wentworth groaned and weaved his head as he moved unsteadily toward the two FUL flunkies.

"What the fuck?!" the black thug said with astonishment. "Where the hell did he come from?"

"Must've been crashed out in the basement," the white hood remarked. "Must be drunk or somethin'."

"Maybe," the other guy remarked as he approached Wentworth. The black man slid a hand inside his jacket. "Hold it right there, ass-wipe."

"I donn . . . I didn't do nuttin'," Wentworth stated in a

slurred voice as he leaned against the wall opposite the basement door.

"You'd better do some explaining, fella," the white thug declared, stepping toward Wentworth, "or your health is gonna get real bad, real fast."

"We ain't just fuckin' around, either," the black guy added as he started to draw a revolver from shoulder leather.

A wire loop suddenly swung over his head. The FUL henchman didn't even hear the basement door creak as Caine stepped silently from the threshold and wrapped the wire saw around the man's neck. The merc yanked the ends of the improvised garrote to tighten the wire across the goon's throat.

"One hard twist and I'll cut your head off," Caine warned. "Raise your hands in front of you, shoulder-width apart, and don't try any tricks."

The other flunky was startled by Caine's unexpected arrival, but he handled it fairly well. The man stepped back and reached for his gun. He didn't see Wentworth twist the ring at the handle of his umbrella. The lieutenant yanked the handle and drew the ten-inch-long icepicklike blade from the Atlanta Cutlery sword umbrella. He thrust the sharp tip under the second thug's chin. The point barely touched the guy's throat.

"Move and I'll perform a very messy tracheotomy," Wentworth warned as he held the sword poised at the gunman's throat. "Very slowly, raise your hands. Try to reach for the sword, or dodge or kick, or any other nonsense, and you'll be whistling through your Adam's apple."

The two FUL henchmen were smart enough to realize they were up against a couple of pros. They knew the two mysterious assailants would probably be familiar with any technique they might attempt to resist, so they surrendered. The mercenaries forced their captives to face each other and place their palms together, fingers interlaced. Wentworth drew his silenced pistol and covered the pair as Caine snapped a pair of thumbcuffs on the thugs.

"Oh, shit," the black guy groaned as his right thumb was locked to the other man's left thumb. "This is embarrassing."

"At least it's not fatal," Caine replied as he snapped on another sent of thumbcuffs to link the left and right thumbs of the thugs' other hands.

"Okay," Wentworth began as he and Caine relieved the pair of their weapons. "We're going down to the basement. Don't do anything stupid or we'll kick you down the stairs and blow your brains out."

The two humiliated hired guns obliged. Caine and Wentworth gagged them and used the hoods' own belts to bind their ankles together and tie them to the furnace. They unloaded the captives' revolvers and left the empty guns on the foot of the stairs, taunting the unlucky thugs and mocking the utter impotence that the two henchmen were experiencing.

Wentworth and Caine checked the hallway before opening the door. Another FUL hoodlum was wandering around the corridor as if looking for a lost dog. A tall, slender man with curly brown hair, the hired gunman seemed confused. He was obviously looking for the two missing jokers whom the mercs had bound to the furnace.

The lanky thug approached the basement door. He reached for the doorknob with one hand and reached inside his jacket for a pistol with the other. Caine drew his knife and waited behind the door. Wentworth moved farther down the stairs and held his silenced Colt in both hands.

The door opened and the gunman peered into the basement. He saw Wentworth with the pistol in his fists. The thug began to draw his gun, but Caine suddenly thrust the blade of his knife under the man's chin and grabbed the hood's wrist to prevent him from drawing his weapon.

"Jesus," the thug rasped through clenched teeth. "I give. Okay?"

The guy realized if Caine and Wentworth wanted him

dead, he already would be bleeding his life away at the head of the stairs. Caine lifted the hood's piece and they marched him down the stairs to join the others. They forced him to sit beside the two captives and cuffed his hands behind his back. Caine used the newest prisoner's belt to tie the guy's manacled wrists to the arms of the other pair. Then he removed the fishing line from the survival kit in the hollow handle of his knife and tied a noose around the man's neck.

"I advise you fellows not to struggle or move around too much," he remarked as he looped the twenty-foot line around the neck of the back man. "This is high-density nylon cord, tested at eight-hundred-pound pull. That means you could all strangle yourselves before the line will break."

He made another noose with the remaining length of the line and slipped it over the third man's head. The three captives appeared more frustrated than frightened, but none of them wanted to find out if their captors would actually kill them. Wentworth and Caine left the trio and mounted the stairs once more.

They checked the corridor. It was empty. The mercs moved to the side door. No guard was posted at the inside, although two FUL flunkies stood in the alley outside. Wentworth took the walkie-talkie from his belt and contacted "Desert Fox."

William O'Neal and Joe Fanelli had positioned themselves across the street from the Munroe Theater. Wentworth's newest radio report had told them the situation. O'Neal and Fanelli had already spotted the two FUL enforcers in the alley. None of Glover's people were stationed at the front of the building and no one was in the limousine. In fact, there were virtually no witnesses near the alley, although a local TV crew had arrived to cover the rally and had just gone inside. Glover must have given them permission to cover the story directly. After all, the TV exposure wouldn't hurt the cult.

The two men in the alley seemed rather bored. They were exchanging obscene jokes as O'Neal and Fanelli approached. The mercs wore loose-fitting sports jackets, dark glasses, wide-brim hats, and false mustaches. They bound Scotch tape around their fingers to prevent leaving prints, in case the plan went sour. The men in the alley stiffened as the two mercs drew closer.

"Hi," O'Neal greeted, holding a clipboard at his chest. "We're with *The Sacramento Insider*. Mind if we ask you fellas a few questions?"

"Yeah," said a heavyset guy who resembled a block of cement dressed up in pinstripe. "We mind."

"No comment, okay?" the other character said quickly.

"Hell," Fanelli began, fumbling with a bulky camera bag, which hung from a shoulder strap. "We're just trying to cover this story from a different angle. Wouldn't you like to tell people what it's like to work for Harold Glover and the FUL?"

"You guys ain't reporters," the block of concrete growled. "Fuck off before you get hurt . . ."

"Take it easy, Frank," the other cult enforcer urged. "You two better take off now."

The side door opened behind the two FUL guards. Wentworth extended an arm, the silenced Colt pistol in his fist. The Hard Corps lieutenant coughed softly to draw the attention of the guards. The two thugs turned and saw the black muzzle of the sound-suppressor pointed in their direction.

"Well, I'll be damned," Fanelli said cheerfully as he extracted his own silenced .45 from the camera bag. "I've got one just like that."

The goons slowly raised their hands in surrender. O'Neal and Fanelli shoved the pair against a wall and ordered them to assume the position. The hoods stood spread-eagled and O'Neal frisked them, confiscated their weapons, and cuffed their wrists behind their backs. Then they escorted the hoods through the door.

"We've got some of your friends down in the basement," Wentworth informed them. "You can come along quietly and join them or we'll kill you right here and now. What's your decision?"

"Let's go meet our friends," the more intelligent of the two men replied. His partner, Frank the cement block, voiced no different opinion.

Caine and Fanelli took the pair to the basement while O'Neal and Wentworth walked through the corridor, heading toward the sound of applause. Since Wentworth was familiar with the theater, O'Neal allowed him to lead the way. They slowly approached a series of doors located behind the stage curtains.

Thor Ornjarta and another FUL enforcer stood near the curtains. They were watching Harold Glover onstage. A pair of binoculars hung from Thor's neck. He occasionally raised the field glasses to his eyes and scanned the audience. The other thug seemed bored with the task. He said something to Thor and the big redhead nodded in reply.

O'Neal and Wentworth saw the flunky head toward the doors. They ducked behind a drinking fountain as the thug opened a door and stepped inside a room. Wentworth recalled that the door led to a rest room, which was used as a general storage area and contained brooms, mops, buckets, and some cartons with a few empty beer bottles. The hood had probably gone inside to take a leak.

"I'll take that one," Wentworth whispered. "Can you handle the freak with the red hair?"

"I'll manage," O'Neal assured him.

Wentworth waited until Thor was checking the audience with the binoculars before he darted to the rest room. The lieutenant opened the door and ducked inside, silenced .45 Colt in his fist. O'Neal covered his partner, watching the big redhead, who was still stationed by the curtains at the edge of the stage.

Another wave of applause signaled the end of Glover's speech. O'Neal hadn't paid much attention to what the Australian cult leader was talking about. It didn't matter anyway because Glover was a goddamn liar. O'Neal was more interested in other sounds, sounds which might pose a threat. He watched Thor from the edge of the curtains. The Swede checked his watch and glanced about the corridor. O'Neal suspected the top FUL enforcer sensed something was wrong and was beginning to wonder where all his men had gone.

Suddenly, O'Neal realized someone had stepped next to him. The Hard Corps commander almost lashed out with the Colt pistol in his fist before he recognized Steve Caine. O'Neal clenched his teeth and glared at the other merc. Caine offered a slight, apologetic shrug. His Katu training had taught him to move with catlike silence. Stealth had become second nature to Caine and he often startled his own teammates without meaning to do so.

"Bloody hell," Glover remarked as he stepped offstage to join Thor. "An excellent speech, if I do say so."

"I think we'd better leave right now," Thor replied. "Something's going on in this theater . . ."

Glover scoffed at his bodyguard. "You think the place is haunted, do you?"

"Boo!" O'Neal announced as he stepped into view with his pistol held in a firm two-hand grip.

Caine followed his example. Both mercenaries aimed their weapons at Thor. The Swede's hand had been inside his suit jacket even before they appeared, but he drew his pistol slowly and held the butt with thumb and forefinger. Caine gestured for Thor to turn around. The big man obliged and Caine stepped forward to take the 9-mm Detonics VI automatic from his hand.

"Put your hands on top of your head and get down on your knees," Caine instructed. "Try anything and I'll put a bullet through the back of your skull."

Harold Glover turned to face William O'Neal. The merc leader pointed his gun at Glover. The Aussie seemed remarkably cool, dressed in his white slacks and shirt, a grin still fixed on his tanned face. Yet, Glover's eyes, firm and strong a moment earlier, revealed he was confused and a little afraid. Nonetheless, O'Neal was surprised. He'd expected to see more fear appear in Glover's face. Anyone with any sense would be frightened when suddenly confronted by an armed assailant. Glover was tougher than he looked.

"If this is robbery," Glover began in a steady voice, "you're not going to get enough money to make it worth all this trouble. If it's a kidnapping, maybe we can deal right now."

"Neither one," O'Neal stated as he raised the gun to point the pistol directly at Glover's face. The grin disappeared from the cult leader's lips. "Right now you're about three centimeters away from death. All I have to do is squeeze the trigger."

"There must be a reason for this," Glover began. "Maybe there's some misunderstanding . . ."

"Looks like you need some better security, Glover," O'Neal remarked. "What you have isn't very good. We went through them without a hitch. A man in your position should hire professionals instead of just dumb muscle."

"Don't trust them, Harry," Thor warned as Caine handcuffed the big man's wrists behind his back.

"Nobody's talking to you," Caine said, jabbing the muzzle of his silenced Colt against the back of Thor's head. "So shut up."

"What is this?" Glover asked. "A job interview? You blokes want to be my bodyguards?"

"We'll talk about that later," O'Neal replied. "You ought to know a little more about us. Remember the Lucifer's motorcycle gang? We wasted those trash—with a little inept help from this muscle-bound faggot who sent some trigger-happy morons who can only hold their own against people who can't shoot back."

"If I knew what you were talking about, I wouldn't admit it," Glover said. "So what's the point to this?"

"Oh, you'll find out," O'Neal said with a smile beneath his false mustache. "We'll meet again, Glover, and then we'll make everything *very* clear."

Wentworth emerged from the rest room. He bowed a

mock greeting to Glover and headed down the corridor to make certain Fanelli didn't need any help. O'Neal gestured for Caine to follow the lieutenant. The tall bearded merc departed and O'Neal himself started to back away from the cult leader.

"Right now," O'Neal concluded, "you just remember this conversation and remember how vulnerable you really are. If we want to take you out, we can do it any damn time we please."

"Hey, big mouth," Thor began as he glanced over his shoulder at O'Neal, "you want to see something?"

The Swede's big shoulders rose and his fists trembled as he pulled his wrists against the handcuffs. A steel link snapped and Thor's arms swung free, metal manacles still attached to his wrists. He glanced back at O'Neal and smiled, but he still remained on his knees.

"Cute," O'Neal remarked, pretending he hadn't been impressed by Thor's demonstration of physical strength. "Now let me show *you* something."

O'Neal lowered the aim of his Colt and squeezed the trigger. The silenced pistol rasped harshly and a big 230-grain bullet splintered wood from the floor between Thor's feet. The Swede gasped and landed on all fours.

"You mess with me, muscle boy, and you'll be on your way to queenie heaven," O'Neal scoffed. He figured Thor probably wasn't gay, but the remarks were meant to upset the Swedish thug. "Glover, you just remember what I told you. Until next time, gentlemen."

The Hard Corps hastily filed out the side door of the Munroe Theater. They concealed their firearms and stepped into the crowd of young people who were emerging from the front of the building. They kept moving down the street until they reached the Toyota van parked a block away. The mercenaries entered the vehicle and removed their disguises.

"Well," Fanelli remarked as he started the engine, "I

guess everything went pretty much as you planned it, Captain. I just hope Glover reacts the way you figure he will."

"Me, too," O'Neal confessed. "If he doesn't, we'll just have to think of something else."

CHAPTER 8

"ARE YOU SERIOUS?" Carol Henderson asked, staring at William O'Neal as if she suspected he might have brain damage. "You really went to the FUL rally and did what you described? You just threatened Glover and think that's going to help?"

O'Neal felt awkward as he sat on the sofa in Carol's neat little living room. She was seated across from him in a Colonial-style arm chair. A coffee table separated them. Carol had placed a quaint blue and white teapot with matching cups on the tabletop. Yet, O'Neal noticed Carol wasn't all that old-fashioned. Copies of *U.S. News & World Report*, *Psychology Today*, and *Time* shared space on the coffee table with the tea set. Carol also had a home computer on a desk at the other side of the room.

The Hard Corps commander was accustomed to facing the most dangerous and difficult tasks with confidence and decisive determination. Yet he felt uncomfortable and un-certain of himself alone with Carol Henderson. O'Neal could not explain this sensation. He wasn't exactly inex-perienced with women, although he'd always been pretty fastidious about the ladies he associated with.

Carol wasn't anybody's idea of a vamp. Slender, though with interesting breasts, her figure was pleasant, but not spectacular. She wore little makeup and favored loose-fitting slacks and blouses with long sleeves and high collars. O'Neal wasn't sure why she appealed to him, but he found her more intriguing than any woman he'd met in quite a while.

"Mr. Jones, or whatever your real name is," Carol continued, "would you please answer my questions? A lot of the other parents are waiting to hear a progress report from me and I'd like to be able to tell them something more positive than what I've just heard."

"Okay," O'Neal began, sipping what remained of the tea in his cup. He managed not to grimace, although he hadn't been able to stomach tea since Vietnam. "We didn't confront Glover just to make some macho threats. The idea is to convince the guy to leave the country for a while."

"What?" Carol asked, still confused. "Why would you want Glover to leave? He'll probably just move to another state or possibly flee to Australia."

"We're hoping he'll do the latter," O'Neal explained. "You see, we know where the Fellowship of Ultimate Living has its base here in California, but we haven't been able to learn where the real FUL headquarters in Australia are located. If we're going to crush the cult and free the kids already in the FUL and hopefully track down those being used as dope mules or sold into white slavery, we'll have to raid both bases."

"You're planning to go to Australia and attack the FUL base there?" Carol asked with astonishment. "I'm beginning to have some doubts about your group, Mr. Jones. This sounds like a con game of some sort. Your men need to raid the cult here in California and then fly over to the land down under to finish the job. So naturally, you'll need more money?"

"I didn't say anything about more money," O'Neal replied.

"Not yet," Carol said with a nod as she leaned back in

her chair and crossed her long legs. "But you certainly realize our little parents' association is a collection of desperate, potentially very emotionally vulnerable people. You probably see me as an over-the-hill gray-haired old lady obsessed with the death of my daughter. Sounds like a pretty easy person to con, right? After all, we certainly can't go to the police and admit we hired a group of mercenaries if you fail to uphold your end of the deal."

"Look, Carol," O'Neal began as he rose from the sofa and moved around the coffee table. "I already told you folks that you don't owe us any money unless we get results. So far we haven't got much to show you what we've accomplished, but that's going to change. Hopefully your opinion about me and the value of my word will change, too."

"I didn't mean to offend you," Carol assured him. She uncrossed her legs and rose from the chair. O'Neal was moving closer and she wasn't sure what the mysterious merc commander might have in mind. "But I've got to keep the parents' association together, and—"

"And you sure guessed wrong about what I see when I look at you," O'Neal declared as he seized her shoulders and pulled her forward.

Carol gasped as he pressed her body against his. She was too startled to react when his lips met her mouth. O'Neal embraced her and kissed harder. She tried to push him away, but O'Neal was too strong. Carol moved her head from side to side to try to break free of his kiss, but O'Neal's head followed hers and braced a hand at the back of her neck to hold her still.

O'Neal grasped her firmly, yet he took care not to hurt her. Carol sensed his passion and felt the fire in his kiss. It frightened her, although she realized he didn't intend to rape her. Almost without meaning to, Carol returned his embrace and slid her tongue into his mouth.

He released her. Carol stepped back, still taken off-guard by his actions. She suddenly swung an open palm across the side of his face. The slap resounded in the quiet room. Carol's mouth fell open, surprised by her own behavior.

"It was worth it." O'Neal smiled.

"I . . ." She didn't know what to say. "I think you'd better go now."

"If that's what you want," O'Neal agreed. "But I want you to know that I couldn't take that remark that you're supposed to be an 'over-the-hill old lady.' Since the first time I saw you, I've wanted to . . . uh, maybe I should say this differently."

"I'm at least five years older than you," Carol stated.

"What the hell does that have to do with how I feel about you?" O'Neal demanded. "Oh, hell. I'll leave."

He headed for the door, but Carol caught his arm. O'Neal turned to face her. Carol's eyes met his as she raised her hands and placed her fingers at the back of his neck.

"Not just yet," she corrected and placed her lips against his.

They kissed with equal passion. Hands wandered across torsos, feeling the curves of spine and hip. O'Neal ran his fingers around one of Carol's breasts. The nipple was hard as a brass stud. Carol moaned happily and slid a hand between O'Neal's thighs. She felt the hardness of his penis, aware of what it meant.

O'Neal tucked an arm under Carol's thighs and picked her up to lower her slowly to the carpet. They lay on the floor, kissing and stroking with greater zeal. O'Neal peeled off Carol's slacks and caressed her long smooth thighs. She helped him remove his jacket. The sight of the pistol in shoulder leather under his left arm startled her.

"Don't worry," he said, stripping off the holster rig. "I'll put it away."

"For a moment I forgot what you do for a living," Carol remarked, a trace of regret in her voice.

"We were doing so well," O'Neal sighed. "Is it ruined now?"

"Shut up and take your clothes off," Carol said with a grin.

He eagerly obliged. Carol's boldness surprised and delighted him. Soon her head was buried in his crotch, her wide, soft lips licking greedily at the head of his cock. Carol took him in her mouth slowly, an inch at a time until her lips touched his taut balls. Carol held him in her mouth as she sucked eagerly at the length of his quivering prick.

Before O'Neal could reach the brink, Carol straddled him and guided his throbbing hard-on between her thighs. O'Neal sighed with pleasure as he sank slowly into her chamber of love. The woman rocked gently, gradually drawing him deeper inside her. O'Neal braced himself on one hand and sat up to kiss Carol's breasts. His tongue and teeth teased her rigid nipples as he drew on her breasts with his lips.

Their lovemaking slowly reached a peak. Carol, no longer in control, began bouncing and bucking against O'Neal's crotch. He arched his back to thrust himself along with the rhythm of the woman's motion. Carol moaned loudly with excited pleasure as she climaxed. O'Neal held back until Carol reached a second orgasm before allowing himself to come.

Carol sprawled across his chest and O'Neal held her close, aware that women place great value on being embraced and caressed after making love. They lay together for about half an hour. Neither said much.

"It's been a long time," Carol eventually admitted, snuggled against his side. "And it was better than I remembered."

"I sure wasn't disappointed," O'Neal assured her. "You're quite a woman, Carol."

"I'm not sure what kind of man you are," she replied. "I don't even know your real name, 'Mr. Jones.' And I don't know why you're a mercernary."

"That's a long story," O'Neal answered. "The reason is probably Vietnam. I learned how to be a soldier in 'Nam. I was a commanding officer of an elite group of fighting men. That's a very special situation. There's nothing else quite like it. I liked it. The camaraderie, the excitement. Hell, even the danger."

"Vietnam was a long time ago," Carol reminded him.

"For some people," O'Neal stated. "When I came back from 'Nam, everybody treated me like a leper. You'd think I was a goddamn war criminal accused of burning women and kids. That's how a lot of Americans viewed Vietnam vets back in the seventies. People thought we were all psychotic or drug addicts. Some people hated us because we went to 'Nam and obeyed orders. Others hated us because we 'lost the war.' Actually, we didn't lose. It was too complicated to just say we won or we lost. Things just got screwed up. But what broke my heart was that the people we fought the war for wouldn't give us the goddamn time of day." He paused for a moment. "All those buddies of mine who died in 'Nam. For what?"

"A lot of people wondered about that," Carol commented. "But why'd you become a mercernary?"

"Because everything, quite frankly, Carol, was shit when I came back to the States and tried to fit into civilian life," O'Neal answered. "It was hard to get a job and even tougher to stay with it. Everything seemed dead, as if the high point of my life was back there in the jungles and rice paddies. Well, the majority of guys who came back from 'Nam adjusted to civilian life and they're doing fine as respected members of society. I didn't. Neither did my three partners. Maybe we're crazy, after all. I don't know, but we function best on a battlefield. Mercs get to fight more wars than other soldiers and they can choose the battlefields they want to fight on. They can also pick their causes and their employers. All I can say is, I'm sure glad we picked you."

"I don't know how I feel about it now," Carol admitted. "I didn't expect anything like this to happen."

The telephone rang. Carol rose and padded barefoot to the phone. O'Neal followed the curves of her ass across the room. She answered the phone and a man's voice asked if "Mr. Jones" was there. Carol gave the phone to O'Neal.

"Yeah," O'Neal spoke into the mouthpiece.

"Got a message from a friend with connections to the airlines," James Wentworth's voice informed O'Neal. "The gentleman from Australia has booked a flight back home. He's departing at twenty-three hundred hours to go back to the land of the kangaroos."

"Okay," O'Neal replied. "I'll meet you in about an hour. Same place we discussed earlier."

"We're looking forward to it," Wentworth assured him.

O'Neal hung up and reached for his clothes.

"Glover's responding the way we'd hoped," he told Carol. "That means I have to get back to work immediately."

"What are you going to do?" Carol asked. She was sitting cross-legged in the chair again, but she was still naked.

"I'm going to give your parents' association evidence that they're getting their money's worth," O'Neal replied as he pulled on his pants. "Hopefully we'll have some good news for you within twelve hours."

CHAPTER 9

THE CALIFORNIA CHAPTER of the Fellowship of Ultimate Living was located far to the north of Fresno. Much of Northern California is still forest and the area is far less populated than the better-known and more active southern portion of the state. The FUL needed a quiet, remote area for their cult base in America. They found it in a lonely sheep farm that had folded up in 1983. The FUL had purchased the land and converted the farm into a "retreat" for the cult.

The Hard Corps were familiar with the site. They'd formerly conducted surveillance on the retreat before the motorcycle gang had given them their first solid lead concerning the secret activities of the cult. The mercenaries had successfully spied on the FUL base by using special light-density telescopes while hidden at the treeline of a forest of evergreens located more than a mile from the cult setup. The Hard Corps had returned to their former surveillance point to check the activity of the FUL that night.

Steve Caine and Joe Fanelli had arrived at the forest shortly after the Hard Corps had encountered Harold Glover at the Munroe Theater. The two merc NCOs had the telescopes set up and were taking turns watching the cult base before O'Neal and Wentworth arrived at 2200 hours.

"Anything interesting going on down there?" O'Neal inquired as he approached the telescopes.

"Glover left about half an hour ago, Captain," Fanelli remarked as he poured himself some coffee. "Rode out in his fancy white limo followed by a bus full of FUL followers who are also going to Australia."

"How do you know they're not going to be sent south of the border to the drug czars and white slavers?" O'Neal inquired.

"Because Glover got airline tickets for twenty-six people simultaneously," Caine answered, stepping away from a telescope. "Even got group rates for taking so many people on his 'Australian tour.' Son of a bitch must have had everybody take care of passports and visas in advance."

"I'm going to have to ask McShayne how he managed to get tapped into the computers at the right airline," O'Neal commented. "That was impressive enough, and sorting out the data this quickly is even better."

"McShayne didn't do it," Wentworth told the team leader. "Somebody else came through with the information. Somebody we didn't think would help us with this mission."

"Old Saintly?" O'Neal asked with surprise. The other men nodded in response. "Well, I'll be damned. Wonder how he managed it."

"My guess is the FBI actually got the data about the airlines and Glover's tour," Wentworth replied. "CIA has computer taps and listening devices in most FBI headquarters around the country. Saintly probably got the information from one of those sources."

"We'll have to send him a nice thank-you card in invisible ink after this is over," O'Neal remarked as he peered into the eyepiece of the telescope.

The special fiber-optics lenses magnified faint reflected light on objects to present a clear image at night. The shapes were various shades of green and yellow, but after one became accustomed to this the light-density telescopes were very easy to use. The FUL base didn't look much different than when the Hard Corps had been conducting regular surveillance on the place two weeks before.

A ten-foot-high steel-wire fence surrounded the retreat. The area consisted of 150 acres of grassland. Some of the land had been tilled and fertilized to grow vegetable gardens for the cult members. The Fellowship of Ultimate Living had apparently insisted that their followers be vegetarians.

It was hard to imagine what the original farmhouse and barn had been like, since both structures had been torn down when the cult purchased the land. Two large wooden billets had been constructed on the site. These housed the current members of the FUL, all the kids who had unsuspectingly stepped into the spider's parlor. A mansion of white brick with a red tile roof was the actual headquarters building at the base. This was Glover's home while in America. Although the cult leader was gone, at least two dozen of his henchmen remained at the base. Most would be inside the head-shed.

The Hard Corps had noted the security of the cult base was designed only to keep people in, with little or no regard for keeping anyone out. The fence was illuminated by tall gooseneck floodlamps mounted on aluminum stalks, but the light shone only on the inside of the fence. A closed-circuit television-surveillance camera was installed above the porch roof over the entrance of the headquarters building.

"Still no sentries posted," O'Neal commented, examining the enemy base through the telescope. "Of course, if they're only concerned with keeping the kids inside the fence, I guess they don't need to post guards. They can detect anybody trying to run to the fence by using television monitors. There must be other cameras in there."

"Oh, yeah," Caine confirmed. "There are cameras posted outside the fence. Four of them. Fixed cameras encased in Plexiglas. No problem. We'll only need to take out one. The other three aren't in position to see anything from the angle that we'll advance from."

"Okay," the Hard Corps leader began. "This is fairly simple, but that doesn't mean it'll be easy. Basically, we just need to take out the bastards in the house. Now, don't forget there may be some innocent kids in there, too. Try not to shoot any innocent bystanders."

"I just hope they didn't manage to brainwash any of those kids bad enough to be conditioned into killers," Fanelli commented. "God knows what they've been doing to those kids in there."

"You've seen too much television," Wentworth snorted. "Besides, trying to turn those kids into killers would be dangerous for the cult enforcers. No way of being sure whom they'd turn their weapons against. That's the problem one encounters when trying to mess with people's heads."

"Sure hate to get in there and find out you're wrong," Fanelli muttered with annoyance.

"Let's get ready," O'Neal instructed. "Time is as big an enemy as the cult. Besides, I'm sick of handling these sons of bitches with kid gloves. Time to put on the brass knuckles."

"That'll be a pleasure," Fanelli agreed, his mood immediately improving at the prospect of kicking the asses of some creeps who richly deserved a leather enema.

The Hard Corps had already donned tiger-stripe camouflage fatigue uniforms to blend with the forest. Every man carried a .45 pistol, grenades, and ammo pouches. O'Neal and Fanelli were armed with Uzi submachine guns. The Hard Corps commander also carried a set of bolt cutters and Fanelli brought along a small "butt-pack" containing plastic explosives as well as the .357 backup piece in shoulder leather.

Wentworth and Caine carried M-16 assault rifles with Starlite night scopes. The mercenary lieutenant also had his *wakazashi* short sword thrust in his gun belt, and Caine was once again armed with his bamboo bow and quiver of arrows. Of course, the tall bearded merc also carried his ever-present survival knife. The four men checked their equipment and briefly discussed strategy before they headed down the hill.

As Caine had previously stated, the mercenaries only had to put one of the outside surveillance cameras out of order. Since the camera was facing the base instead of the hill, they didn't have to worry about it until they reached the fence. O'Neal simply draped a canvas tarp over the Plexiglas shell that encased the camera to put the device out of commission.

The Hard Corps moved on to the fence. Though the other three fence cameras were harmless, the rotating TV camera on the porch roof of the mansion still presented a problem.

"You sure you can put an arrow through the fence and hit the target accurately?" O'Neal whispered to Caine.

"I'll have to get closer to be sure," Caine replied as he drew a target arrow from his quiver.

"Wait a second," Fanelli urged as he knelt by the fence. "I found a wire hidden by the grass at the bottom of the fence."

"Is it electrified or an alarm system?" O'Neal asked.

"It's an alarm," Fanelli replied with a positive nod. "Wrong kind of wiring for an electric fence. We'd better take care of this before Steve does his Robin Hood act. If an arrow scrapes the fence it could set off the alarm."

"Will the cables put it out?" Wentworth asked.

"I sure hope so," Fanelli answered as he extracted a six-foot-long rubber cable from a pouch by his left hip. He unwound the cord and pressed the alligator clips at each end of the cable. "Need a hand here."

"Okay," O'Neal said as he knelt beside Fanelli and took one end of the cable.

Fanelli held the other end and they stretched out the cable. Wentworth and Caine watched the enemy base, weapons held ready, while the other two mercs opened the alligator clips and moved the metal teeth toward the wire.

"Ready?" Fanelli inquired. O'Neal nodded. "Now."

Both Fanelli and O'Neal closed the clips on the wire at the same time. This neutralized the electrical flow of the wire between the clips. Fanelli took a NATO push-button knife from his pocket. He pressed the button and a five-inch steel blade snapped into place. The merc used the sharp edge to sever the wire near each clip.

"Okay," Fanelli said, a trace of strain in his voice. "That ought to do it. Unless this is a trickier alarm than it appears to be, it ought to be deactivated. If I'm wrong, then it means we've already set off a silent alarm inside and the enemy knows we're here."

"Guess we'll find out real soon," O'Neal remarked. He turned to Steve Caine. "Take out the camera."

Caine notched the arrow to his bowstring and drew it back. He aimed carefully and slid the metal tip of the target arrow through a space in the wire fence. Caine released the missile and watched the arrow jet across the compound. It struck the side of the revolving camera. The shaft blocked the motion of the camera and locked it in place by forming a solid bar between camera and the ledge of the porch roof.

"Nice shot," Fanelli remarked.

"It was okay," Caine said with a modest shrug.

O'Neal raised the bolt cutters and clipped segments of the wire fence. He worked the handles as the heavy blades of the cutters snipped through the thick steel wire. O'Neal cut as quickly as possible until he'd severed a three-foot square in the fence. A hard kick knocked the improvised "door" from the barrier.

The Hard Corps boss stepped aside and allowed Steve Caine to slither through the hole first. The others slid through one by one, passing their weapons through the opening before crawling through to the inside of the enemy base.

"So far so good," Wentworth commented as he gathered

up his M-16 and braced the plastic stock against a hip, the barrel pointed toward the house.

"Steve," O'Neal began, "check out the back. Joe, come with me. Cover us, Lieutenant."

Wentworth nodded and assumed a kneeling stance with his rifle held ready. Caine headed for the rear of the house while O'Neal and Fanelli moved to the front entrance. The night seemed unnaturally quiet and a cold wind stroked their flesh as if the breath of the Grim Reaper were blowing down upon them.

Caine approached the rear of the building cautiously, creeping through the shadows beneath the overhang of the roof. He saw a door open and two men emerge. Caine froze in a crouched position, aware that people tend to ignore objects in darkness unless a shape moves. The pair approached him, apparently unaware of his presence.

One man carried a canvas tool bag in one hand while his other fist held the shoulder strap to a Smith & Wesson Model 76 submachine gun, which hung by his right hip. The other guy carried a stainless-steel Mini-14 semiautomatic rifle at port arms. Caine guessed they had been sent to check on the cameras and make repairs. The firepower was in case they encountered a problem that involved more than short circuits.

The FUL enforcers walked past Caine without knowing he was there. The merc dropped his bow and drew the survival knife from leather. He attacked the man with the rifle because the opponent with a weapon in hand presented the greater threat. The gunman opened his mouth to cry out as Caine seized him from behind.

Caine's left hand grabbed the man's lower face, covering his mouth as he pulled him backward. The merc's right hand drove the knife upward. The steel tip pierced the junction at the base of the hoodlum's skull, where the spinal cord meets the brain stem. The blade severed the vital life link and stabbed into the medulla oblongata of the brain. The man was dead before he could realize what happened.

The knife was lodged in the man's skull, the sawtooth side of the blade caught on bone. Caine discarded the corpse with the knife still buried in the dead man's skull. The second cult flunky dropped the canvas tool bag and grabbed for his S&W subgun.

Caine lunged forward, drawing an arrow from the quiver on his back. He plunged the steel tip of the hunting broadhead of the arrow into the thug's chest and grabbed the M-76. Caine pushed the barrel aside with one hand and grabbed the man's fist, which was wrapped around the pistol grip of the submachine gun. The mercenary held the man's index finger braced against the trigger guard to prevent the gunman from firing the weapon.

The curare-laced arrow rapidly took effect. The poison took over muscles and nerves. An ugly gurgle escaped from the dying man's throat as paralysis gripped his windpipe and vocal cords. He raised his free arm slowly, fingers arched into a frozen claw. The man's body jerked in a weak spasm as his heart stopped. Caine pried the thug's finger from the trigger guard of the M-76 and shoved his opponent to the ground. The man twitched once more and ceased moving forever.

"Life is tough," Caine whispered as he glanced down at the body. "So is death."

O'Neal and Fanelli stepped onto the porch and stood by the door. Wentworth remained well behind them in order to cover the pair. Fanelli tried the doorknob. It turned easily and Fanelli pulled the door. He didn't open it, but he nodded to O'Neal to let the mercenary leader know the door wasn't locked. O'Neal readied his Uzi and nodded in return.

Movement at the porch roof drew Wentworth's attention upward. A man slid open a second-story window and slithered onto the porch roof with a CAR-15 in his grasp. *Bastard must have noticed the arrow sticking from the camera,* Wentworth thought as he raised his M-16. The mercenary officer snap-aimed, braced the assault rifle against a hip, and squeezed the trigger. A trio of 5.56-mm slugs hissed from the muzzle of the foot-long noise suppressor attached to the threaded barrel.

The gunman grunted methodically three times, once for each bullet that slammed into his chest. The man's heart was ripped apart, but as he died he managed to pull the trigger to his CAR-15. The carbine spat a wild volley of unmuffled full-auto gunshots into the night sky as the dead man tumbled off the porch roof and plunged to the hard earth below.

Alarmed voices erupted from within the mansion. The sound of shoe leather slapping floorboards warned O'Neal and Fanelli that the enemy had been alerted by the gunshots, and two or more were headed toward the door.

Fanelli yanked open the door at the precise moment a cult enforcer on the opposite side reached for the knob. The tough Italian from Jersey glimpsed the man's startled face a split second before he smashed the steel frame of his Uzi into it. The hoodlum tumbled backward, blood oozing from a crushed nose. He fell into the path of another thug who was trying to point an M-3 submachine gun at the mercenaries at the open door. The man's aim was knocked off target and he fired a harmless volley of .45 rounds into the ceiling.

Joe Fanelli promptly trained his Uzi on the pair and opened fire. He didn't hesitate even though neither opponent was readily able to shoot back at him. They were bottom-of-the-barrel scum, as bad as any terrorists or professional criminals the Hard Corps had encountered in the past. They deserved no mercy and Fanelli showed them none.

The wave of 9-mm slugs crashed into the two cult goons and sent their bullet-torn corpses sliding across the white tile floor of the hallway within. Other gunmen jumped away from the bodies. Two of them ran for the stairs. Another thug swung an Ingram machine pistol toward the door and fired a spray of 9-mm rounds at Fanelli.

The wiry merc ducked back behind the doorway to

avoid the deadly burst. O'Neal had retreated to the opposite side of the doorway. He poked the barrel of his Uzi
around the corner and triggered a burst of high-velocity
parabellums into the Ingram gunner. The guy's body
seemed to hop backward, blood spitting from a trio of
ragged holes in his chest. The man's body crashed to the
tiles and the MAC-10 skidded from his lifeless fingers.

Fanelli swung his Uzi inside and hosed the stairwell
with a volley of full-auto fury. Bullets splintered sections
of the railing and stair risers. One of the FUL slobs who'd
tried to flee upstairs caught two 9-mm slugs in the legs. He
screamed and tumbled backward down the stairs while his
partner crawled to the solid cover of a banister post at the
landing.

O'Neal darted past Fanelli, running in a low crouched
position. The Hard Corps commander dashed to the foot of
the stairs while Fanelli continued to fire at the gunman's
position at the landing. The thug was pinned down behind
the post as O'Neal moved into position and fired a stream
of 9-mm rounds directly up the stairs.

Parabellum slugs smashed into the gunman's left
shoulder and upper arm. The impact spun him around to
receive more bullets from both O'Neal and Fanelli. The
man's body collapsed across the landing. A pool of blood
formed around what was left of his skull.

"Help me," a voice moaned near O'Neal's boot.

He glanced down at the wounded FUL goon who'd been
shot in the legs by Fanelli before he tumbled down the
stairs. The guy's face was contorted with pain and a bloody
shard of broken bone jutted from his right shin. O'Neal felt
a twinge of pity for the wounded man, who reminded him
of a GI he'd seen buy the farm one hot afternoon when
Hell had rolled into the Muong Xepon.

But that had been along the border of Vietnam and
Laos. The injured man at O'Neal's feet was a slime-bucket
who had helped kids fall into a different kind of hell,
which included drugs, rape, and slavery among its tor-

ments. The bastard deserved to die, but O'Neal wanted to take a couple of the cult enforcers alive for interrogation.

"Fuck you," he snarled as he kicked the man in the face and knocked him unconscious.

Three more gunmen suddenly appeared from a room connected to the hallway. Fanelli whirled and triggered his Uzi, but he had exhausted the ammo from its magazine. The merc swore under his breath and dived to the floor as a salvo of enemy fire blazed above his hurtling form. Fanelli rolled across the floor. Two bullets whined against tile near his position.

O'Neal blasted one of the attackers with his Uzi. The 9-mm slugs ripped into the closest gunman's stomach and chest. A Smith & Wesson subgun flew from the thug's hands as he stumbled into a wall, slid to the floor, and vomited blood across his shirtfront. The remaining two gunmen turned their weapons on O'Neal's position. The merc leader ducked behind the banister post at the foot of the stairs. He flinched as bullets thudded into the thick wood shield and chipped portions of surrounding handrail and risers.

Fanelli had drawn his .45 Colt. He assumed a prone position, held the pistol in both hands, and fired two rounds into the belly of another opponent. The creep shrieked in agony as his stomach and liver were torn into useless globs of pulped tissue. The bastard's gun clattered on the floor; then his trembling body collapsed across it.

The third FUL gunman tried to duck behind the doorway to avoid exposing himself to the mercenaries' fire. He suddenly appeared again and fell to his knees. The man's face twisted in agony before he dropped forward and lay flat on the floor. The shaft of an arrow jutted from his back beneath the left shoulder blade.

"Looks like Steve found another door," Fanelli commented as he holstered his pistol and retrieved his Uzi. "Either that, or there are friendly Indians on our side."

"Tell Wentworth to get in here," O'Neal ordered, changing magazines to his Uzi submachine gun. The Hard Corps leader glanced at the stairwell and the corridor that extended to the east wing of the mansion. He wasn't worried about more attackers coming from the room to the west. Caine had that side covered.

Fanelli moved toward the door, loading a fresh magazine into the well of his Uzi as he moved. Shots erupted outside. He peered through the doorway and saw Wentworth running toward the entrance. The merc lieutenant fired his M-16 as he ran. Wentworth pointed the weapon at a window at the west wing and triggered a quick burst at a rifleman stationed there. Glass shattered and a man's body crashed through the broken framework. The corpse slumped across the sill, upper torso dangling over the edge.

More shots exploded from the porch roof and bullets tore into the ground near Wentworth's feet as he ran for the door. Two or more opponents were stationed on the porch roof, firing pistols at the lieutenant. Fanelli raised his Uzi and blasted a column of bullet holes through the ceiling of the porch roof.

Nine-millimeter 115-grain projectiles pierced the wooden platform. Most of the bullets lost too much energy passing through the roof. They popped harmlessly through the other side like a handful of tossed pebbles. Still, three bullets had enough force to cause some serious damage to the gunmen on the porch roof. One man yelped with pain when a slug burst through the roof under his feet, pierced shoe leather, and tore his foot into a bloody pulp of broken bones and smashed muscle.

Another gunman was even less lucky. Two bullets passed between his legs and drilled directly into his genitals. He uttered a high-pitched shriek and toppled from the porch roof, hitting the ground with a spine-jarring thud. Wentworth jumped onto the porch and slipped inside the house.

"Got another surprise for you fuckers," Fanelli growled as he took an M-26 hand grenade from his belt.

Two bullets tore through the roof, fired by one or more opponents above Fanelli. The projectiles hissed past Fanelli and punched through the floorboards of the porch less than an inch from his foot. The merc yanked the pin from his grenade. He wanted to throw it immediately, but he held the M-26 in his fist and popped the spoon to trigger the fuse.

Fanelli counted "one, two" and leaned forward to hurl the explosive. He tossed it with an underhand throw, lobbing the grenade onto the porch roof. Fanelli quickly dived into the doorway. Another bullet burst from the roof and scraped the heel of Fanelli's right boot as he plunged across the threshold.

The grenade exploded a split second later. The porch roof vanished in a burst of flying splinters and broken tiles. Chunks of human parts were scattered among the debris. Everything fell to earth in a shower of wreckage and gore.

"Thanks for the help, Sergeant," Wentworth remarked as he assisted Fanelli to his feet.

"Sure," Fanelli replied as he tried to catch his breath.

Two figures appeared at the head of the stairs with submachine guns in their fists. The pair pointed their weapons at Fanelli and Wentworth, but O'Neal opened fire before the hoods could trigger their choppers. A wave of Uzi rounds plowed into the closest attacker and ripped a column of bullet holes across his chest. The hoodlum slumped across the risers as his partner screamed and fell against the handrail with two parabellum slugs lodged in his upper torso.

Wentworth raised his rifle and pumped a three-round burst into the wounded gunman. The thug's body jerked wildly from the impact and wiggled over the top of the handrail. His body fell twelve feet to the hard tile floor below. However, three more FUL killers approached from the corridor at the east wing.

Fanelli's Uzi blasted a spray of 9-mm rounds into the advancing trio. One man folded up and crumpled to the floor. Another opponent fell back against a wall, blood oozing from a bullet hole in the hollow of his throat. The third man was sheltered by the bodies of his comrades. He pointed a pump shotgun at Fanelli and fired a burst of buckshot.

The mercenary groaned and spun about as several pellets tore at his upper arm and shoulder. The shotgunner worked the pump action of his 12-gauge blaster to eject a spent shell and chamber a fresh cartridge. Fanelli dropped to one knee and tried to aim the Uzi with one hand, although he realized he was already too late.

A missile blurred as it rocketed above Fanelli's head. The projectile sailed down the corridor and struck the shotgun man in the face. The man's head bounced, a two-foot wooden shaft vibrating from his left eye socket. The arrow had pierced the eyeball to stab deep into his brain. The gunman died on his feet and fell across the bodies of his slain partners.

Fanelli turned toward the west wing and saw Steve Caine lower his bamboo bow. The bearded mercenary discarded the bow and slipped off the empty quiver as he approached Fanelli.

"Remind me never to play darts with you, Steve," Fanelli remarked through clenched teeth. "That shot was showing off a little, don't you think?"

"To be honest," Caine began as he tore open Fanelli's sleeve to examine the buckshot wound, "I rushed the shot and aimed at the guy's chest. Arrow went a little high and to the right."

"No kiddin'?" Fanelli asked, glancing at the blood stains on his shoulder and upper arm. It appeared to be nothing worse than some deep scratches.

"Yeah," Caine confessed. "But don't tell Wentworth."

"How bad is Joe hit?" O'Neal asked with concern, trying to pay attention to the stairs and the corridor while inquiring about his injured teammate.

"I'm okay," Fanelli assured him. "Shit, it ain't nothin'."

"I didn't ask you," O'Neal snapped, aware that Caine would give him a more honest reply under the circumstances. Fanelli would say it was "just a flesh wound" if both his legs had been blown off in a combat situation that was still in progress.

"Doesn't look bad, sir," Caine announced. "In fact, I've seen men with more serious wounds from a tattoo needle."

"Come on," Fanelli groaned. "It's not *that* slight."

"Oh, shut up," Wentworth said. Now that he was certain Fanelli's wound wasn't serious, the lieutenant could make light of it. "You've already got a Purple Heart."

"Patch up Joe as best you can in a hurry," O'Neal ordered. "Joe, can you fight?"

"Damn right I can," Fanelli assured him as Caine opened a first-aid kit and applied a disinfectant cream to the buckshot wound.

"Okay," the team leader declared. "Steve, you and I will take the upstairs. Jim, you and our bulletproof hero check the corridor. We seem to have a lull in the battle, but I don't think the enemy are defeated just because they've cut off the attack."

"Probably waiting for us to come to them now," Wentworth commented as he shoved a fresh magazine into the well of his M-16.

"Well, let's not disappoint them," O'Neal replied.

CHAPTER 10

WILLIAM O'NEAL AND Steve Caine slowly mounted the stairs. O'Neal took the lead, his Uzi pointed ahead of him. Caine followed with his M-16 held ready. The mercenaries breathed deeply, trying to calm their racing hearts. It was a frightening situation, and both men were smart enough and experienced enough to be afraid. More opponents almost certainly lurked upstairs. The enemy had the high ground, and the Hard Corps could only guess how many cult enforcers remained or what they might do next.

O'Neal took a concussion grenade from his belt and unbent the pin in case he needed to pull it out in a hurry. Caine gazed up at the handrail to the upstairs hallway and braced the plastic stock of his M-16 along his hip. Several shapes moved stealthily through the hall. They moved in the shadows fairly well, Caine noted, but the Katu-trained mercenary was an expert in camouflage and stealth. The enemy weren't good enough to avoid his keen eye.

Caine swung the rifle toward the shapes and opened fire. He sprayed the hall with 5.56-mm rounds, more concerned about pinning the enemy down than shooting any particular target. Two more opponents appeared at the head of the stairs. O'Neal drove them back with a volley of Uzi rounds. He held the weapon by the pistol grip in one fist with the folding stock tucked under his arm. He couldn't fire the subgun accurately in this manner, but it was good enough to hold the enemy at bay as he tried to pull the pin from the concussion grenade.

O'Neal gripped the ring in his teeth. Heroes in war films pull the pins from grenades with their teeth all the time, but it's not how the U.S. Army instructs its personnel in basic combat training. O'Neal had never yanked out a grenade pin with his teeth before, and it wasn't so easy— even though he'd loosened the pin in advance. At last, the pin slid free.

The Hard Corps leader hurled the grenade upstairs and sprayed the walls with another quick burst of 9-mm slugs. O'Neal and Caine ducked, covered their ears, and opened their mouths. The grenade exploded. The concussion blast seemed to shake the building; dust and plaster showered down on the two mercenaries. An unconscious and bloodied FUL flunky landed unceremoniously on the stairs next to them.

O'Neal jogged to the top of the stairs. Five more hoods littered the hall. Three were unconscious or dead, blood still dripping from nostrils and ears. Two others were dazed and crawling about on all fours, yet they still had their firearms in hand. O'Neal didn't intend to take any chances with them. He blasted the pair with a lethal salvo of Uzi slugs.

Caine stepped to the summit of the stairs and glanced about the corridor. He saw a door open slightly, just enough for a man to peek out and poke the barrel of a pistol through the gap. Caine snap-aimed his M-16 and fired a hasty burst at the door. Bullets tore into the wall and the doorframe. The ambusher's pistol roared and a bullet screamed between Caine and O'Neal on its path down the hallway.

The bearded merc shoved O'Neal into a wall to keep his commander clear of the gunman's line of fire. Caine dropped to one knee and pointed his rifle at the door, which burst open to reveal the pistolman. He was a heavy-set black guy and stood with his feet shoulder-width apart, both hands wrapped around the butt of his .357 Magnum. It was a standard shooter's stance taught by the military and the police, but it works better on a firing range than against opponents who can shoot back.

The black gunman stood fully exposed as if the proper stance somehow made him bulletproof. Caine showed him the error of this notion by pumping three 5.56-mm slugs through the bastard's chest. The thug uttered a long moan and slid along the door to fall lifeless in the hallway.

"God damn it!" a voice cried from within the room. "I surrender, damn it! Don't shoot! I give up . . ."

"Come out slow," O'Neal shouted in reply. He didn't take time to reload the Uzi, choosing to draw his .45 pistol instead. "Keep your hands up, and I mean *high,* with the fingers spread apart. We'd better be able to count your fuckin' fingers the second you set foot outside that room."

"Okay!" the voice answered. "Don't shoot! I'm comin' out!"

Caine pressed the release catch to his M-16 and dumped the magazine from the well. There were still two cartridges left, but Caine wanted to insert a fresh mag to make certain he had ample firepower. O'Neal gestured for Caine to stay put and cover him. The Hard Corps leader kept his back to the wall as he moved toward the door.

A man stepped from the room. Tall and thin, despite a round pot belly, he was slightly older than the other FUL gunmen the Hard Corps had encountered. His long fingers trembled as he held his hands high and walked unsteadily into the hallway. His thin face was filled with fear and his eyes bulged behind wire-rimmed glasses. O'Neal wasn't sure what the guy did for the cult, but it was hard to believe he was an enforcer.

"I'm not a violent man," the frightened prisoner declared. "I never approved of violence . . ."

"That puts you at a disadvantage," O'Neal told him.

"Because we *do* approve of violence, under the right circumstances. And we've found a lot of the right circumstances going on here."

Suddenly, another figure appeared at the doorway. A big man with a barrel chest and a broad face, he looked more like a regular thug than the trembling dude in the hall. A Remington shotgun in his fists left no room for doubt.

O'Neal's Colt roared before the shotgunner could trigger his weapon. A big 230-grain copper-jacketed bullet crashed into the goon's forehead. The projectile blasted out the back of his skull, brains splattering the doorway. The dead man fell back inside the room, the shotgun still clenched in his fists.

"Oh, Christ," the frightened cult member in the hall gasped. He began shaking worse than before.

"Tried to set us up," Caine commented, glaring at the man.

"He made me do it," the guy replied, his lips trembling so badly he could barely speak well enough to be understood. "He used me for bait. I'm not armed . . ."

'Neal jabbed his left fist into the man's solar plexus. he guy's mouth locked in an egg-shape as he doubled up with a gasp. O'Neal shoved the man to the floor and aimed his pistol at his prisoner's head.

"You got a name, scumbag?" O'Neal asked.

Bowers," the man whimpered. "Maurice Bowers. I'm just a chemist."

You're just a piece of shit as far as I'm concerned," O'Neal told him. "And you'd better come up with a good reason why we shouldn't shoot you full of holes and flush you down the toilet."

What . . . what do you want to know?" Bowers asked in a defeated tone.

James Wentworth and Joe Fanelli moved along the downstairs corridor, searching for any cult enforcers that might remain hidden in the mansion. They encountered a column of doors and began checking them, one by one. The task was nerve-racking because they realized an ambush might lie behind any of the doors.

The mercs approached the first door. They stood at opposite sides of the doorway, weapons held upright. Fanelli stood clear of the door as he slammed a boot under the knob. The lock broke and the door swung inward. The mercs thrust the barrels of their weapons through the opening.

The room was an office with a large walnut desk, surrounded by a semicircle of scoop-backed chairs. The walls were bare and the floor was hard tile. Even the desktop was bare except for a gooseneck lamp and a single white telephone. Wentworth stepped across the threshold while Fanelli covered the hall.

Gunshots and an explosion roared from upstairs. O'Neal and Caine had obviously found some action above. Fanelli started to turn toward the sound, but his chin brushed the freshly bandaged wound on his shoulder. The merc realized he had to concentrate on the corridor for now. The enemy could strike from any direction and Fanelli had to carry out his current part of the team's mission. O'Neal and Caine were on their own for the moment and Fanelli couldn't allow concern about his teammates to distract him from giving one hundred percent.

Wentworth, however, was thinking only of his own survival. A large, muscular thug had positioned himself by the door of the office. When Wentworth entered, the hoodlum grabbed the barrel of his M-16 and pulled hard, trying to wrench the rifle from Wentworth's grasp. Another FUL killer rose from behind the desk with a small, shiny handgun in his fist.

The mercenary officer instantly assessed the situation and reacted to it. The man who tried to pull the rifle from Wentworth's grasp was larger and physically stronger than the merc. Although Wentworth might be able to get the better of the man in a tug-of-war by using superior skill and leverage, the threat from the pistolman meant Wentworth had to act swiftly and with deadly force.

He released the M-16. The startled muscle man staggered backward with the rifle in his fists. Wentworth's *wakazashi* swung from its scabbard in a rapid cross-draw. The samurai short sword struck the hoodlum across the throat. Blood gushed from the deep cut and dyed the man's shirt bright crimson. The thug dropped the rifle and clutched at his slit throat as he wilted to the floor.

The gunman had advanced from the desk and tried to point his little .25-caliber Raven automatic at Wentworth's skull. The small-caliber weapon was obviously the only thing the guy could get his hands on; a .25 auto fires only a small projectile with a weak powder level, and has extremely poor range or potential stopping-power. The guy probably planned to stick the gun in Wentworth's ear before firing it.

Wentworth spun to confront the pistolman. He swung the flat of his sword against the killer's wrist to deflect the aim of the .25 auto. The pistol barked and fired a harmless round into a wall. Wentworth immediately slashed the blade across the gunman's chest and grabbed the handle in a two-hand grip to raise it overhead.

The hoodlum began to scream from the pain of the deep wound across his upper torso. Blood soaked the man's shirt and he fired the .25 auto again, pumping a useless bullet into the tile floor. Wentworth's *wakazashi* struck once more. The razor-sharp edge sliced his opponent's neck, severing the carotid artery and jugular vein. More blood flowed from the FUL hitman as he dropped to the floor and died.

Fanelli heard the battle in the office and prepared to assist Wentworth, but another door suddenly burst open and two hired thugs on the FUL payroll aimed weapons at the Italian kid from Jersey. Fanelli quickly fired his Uzi into the first opponent. The bastard caught three 9-mm slugs in the heart and lungs before he could trigger his Smith & Wesson blast-machine.

The dead man fell against the second hoodlum and knocked a MAC-10 from the guy's hands. The surviving thug immediately shoved his slain partner forward and used the dead man as a combination shield and battering ram. Fanelli tried to dodge the hoodlums, but the live thug pushed his dead partner into the merc. Fanelli's Uzi clattered to the floor. The Hard Corps warrior was driven backward into a wall with the FUL goon at his throat.

Fanelli swung a left hook to his opponent's face. The thug grunted as his head jerked from the punch. Fanelli pushed the man with his right hand and hit him again with a left. The FUL creep was bigger than Fanelli, but the merc was the veteran of a hundred street fights, a hundred savage battlefields.

He rammed a right upper-cut to the big blond thug's stomach. The hood growled and lashed a karate chop to the side of Fanelli's neck. The merc staggered from the blow as pain branched from his neck to fill his head with white-hot agony. The goon then slammed a heel-of-the-palm stroke under Fanelli's jaw. This blow sent Fanelli hurtling backward into the wall. The back of his skull struck the surface and his vision vanished in a burst of lights exploding inside his head.

Fanelli blinked to clear his vision. The blond thug raised an arm, palm cupped, the side of his hand aimed at Fanelli's throat. The hood slashed the deadly karate stroke at the merc, planning to kill Fanelli with one final blow.

Fanelli ducked and slid down the wall to drop to one knee. The hood's hand swung above Fanelli's head and smashed into the wall. The mercenary quickly grabbed his opponent's legs, wrapping his arms around the thug's shins and calves. Fanelli pulled hard and yanked the man's feet from the floor.

The thug crashed down, his back landing hard against the tiles. Fanelli jumped to his feet, bent a knee, and dropped forward. His knee landed in the fallen man's abdomen with all his weight behind it. The hood groaned from the blow and Fanelli smashed a fist in his face.

Fanelli didn't let up. He pinned the goon's arms under his knees and slugged the guy again. Fanelli hammered the

man's face with his fists and hit him with three more hard
punches. The pinned man suddenly bent a knee and raised
it sharply to strike Fanelli in the small of the back.

The thug struggled and managed to buck the stunned
merc off his chest. Fanelli sprawled across the floor and
glanced at the savage, bloodied face of his opponent. The
hood started to rise on all fours. Fanelli braced himself
with his hands and a knee on the floor to lash out with his
other boot. He kicked the thug on the point of the chin.
The man flopped on his back, unconscious.

"You all right?" Wentworth asked as he stepped into the
corridor. The merc lieutenant had retrieved his M-16 and
returned the samurai short sword to its scabbard.

"Did you have fun watchin'?" Fanelli panted, out of
breath, as he climbed to his feet. His head ached and his
wounded shoulder throbbed, but he walked to his Uzi and
gathered up the subgun. "That son of a bitch wasn't a
pushover."

"I noticed," Wentworth agreed. "But I didn't want to
upset you by getting involved in your fight. I know how
proud you are."

"Next time don't worry about hurting my feelings,"
Fanelli replied as he snapped a pair of handcuffs on the
unconscious thug. "Find anything in the office?"

"Ambushers," Wentworth said with a shrug. "We'll
check the desk later. We still have to finish inspecting the
rest of the mansion first."

"It's been a barrel of laughs so far," Fanelli muttered.

The mercenaries checked the last two doors. Each led to
an empty room. However, the rooms were rather intriguing. One was an arms room, filled with rifle racks and gun
cases. Most of these were empty—not surprising, since
the enemy had been using the weapons to try to kill the
Hard Corps. A dozen MP-style black batons were also
mounted in racks along the wall. Some blank spaces suggested more nightsticks were missing from the collection.

"What the hell . . ." Fanelli began as he opened a glass
case holding several rectangular black plastic devices. He

removed one of the contraptions and stared at the metal prongs that jutted from the narrow end.

"Nova stun guns," Wentworth remarked as he examined one of the plastic devices. He pressed a button on the side of the box. A tongue of blue electricity danced across the prongs with a sharp crackle. "It's a nonlethal weapon that you press against an opponent at close quarters. Hits him with approximately forty-thousand volts, but no amps."

"So you can shock the shit outa somebody without taking any risks of causing real injury," Fanelli said with a nod as he tested the stun gun in his fist. Nothing happened. "Guess this one needs to be charged."

"The Nova uses a regular nine-volt battery," Wentworth commented as he put the stun guns back in the case. "These things are sold for self-defense, but I don't think the Fellowship of Ultimate Living has been using them for that purpose."

"I can guess what they've been using the stun guns for," Fanelli said. "Probably helps 'em keep the kids in line."

"Shocking discovery," Wentworth remarked, poker-faced.

Fanelli groaned at the pun and they moved on to the next room. It proved to be a laboratory with racks of test tubes, beakers, microscopes, and jars of assorted chemicals. The lab wasn't much different from what one might find in a high school chemistry class, except for two large vats containing white powder of different textures.

"Baking powder," Wentworth remarked as he placed a small dab of powder from one vat on the tip of his tongue.

"Holy shit!" Fanelli exclaimed, testing a tiny sample from the other vat. "This is coke—and pretty fucking pure coke if you ask me. Bet they've got a few million dollars of it around here."

"They're making crack here," Wentworth said as he studied the lab. Further inspection revealed another vat, which contained dried ground leaves similar to tobacco. Fanelli stepped forward, pinched some leaves between his fingers, and inhaled. A sly smile slid across his face.

"Demon weed," he announced. "Good old mari-hoo-chie."

"I figured you'd recognize it," Wentworth said dryly.

"Hell, Lieutenant," Fanelli replied. "I quit smokin' this shit even before I gave up booze. But this is pretty high-grade stuff. Mexican, Colombian, could even be from Hawaii. Guess they're dealin' grass as well as crack. I bet they get the kids to sell this shit. It's a lot easier to sell grass than crack—though I bet crack's catching up these days."

The two mercs moved out of the lab. Wentworth had his M-16 ready. "Too bad we have to leave that stuff for evidence," Wentworth said. "I'd like to destroy it."

"Somebody probably will later," Fanelli replied as they moved down the hall. "But there's so much drugs available, the only real way to stop it will be when people finally decide not to buy the crap."

"One problem at a time, Joseph," Wentworth told him as they approached a room at the end of the corridor.

It was a large dining room with a long oak table and matching chairs. No one was lurking behind the furniture so the mercs headed for the next room. It was a kitchen with two large freezers, two electrical ovens, and a big refrigerator. A dead hoodlum lay on the tile floor with an arrow lodged in his chest.

"Well, what do you know," Wentworth commented. "Caine left his calling card."

"Yeah," Fanelli said as he glanced about the kitchen. "Guess we've come full circle. Still, there's only three buildings here and the FUL sure wouldn't be using the kids' billets for the white slavery and dope business. I bet—"

The merc stopped in mid-sentence as he noticed an OUT OF ORDER sign posted on the big steel door to one of the freezers. Fanelli approached it and slipped off his small pack of plastic explosives. Wentworth nodded as he stepped beside the door.

"They have a lot of people here," Fanelli remarked as

he grabbed the handle of the freezer door. "But not enough to need two room-size freezers. And . . . I thought so. This sucker is locked from the inside."

"We didn't find a basement door either," Wentworth added. "Although there may not be a basement."

"I think maybe we found it," Fanelli stated as he opened the pack and removed a block of C-4 plastique.

The Hard Corps demolition expert broke off a small portion of the white doughlike plastic explosive. Composition Four is very powerful, twenty times more powerful than TNT. Fanelli needed only a couple of ounces, which he carefully inserted in the doorjamb near the handle. Fanelli stuck a special blasting cap and detonator in the C-4 charge.

"Go in the dining room for a minute, Lieutenant," he told Wentworth. "Don't want you catching any shrapnel."

"No argument there, Sergeant," Wentworth assured him as he moved to the next room.

Fanelli attached the wires to an electrical squib to the detonator. He unwound the wires as he moved to the cover of a stove. Fanelli sat behind the stove and pressed the button to the squib. The C-4 exploded, blasting the lock. The door popped open.

"Knock, knock!" Fanelli shouted as he pointed his Uzi at the opening. "Come on out, you motherfuckers!"

Wentworth approached with his M-16 pointed at the door. Fanelli gestured for the lieutenant to stay back. Wentworth stepped behind the open door and raised his rifle barrel toward the ceiling.

"If you don't come out we'll toss some grenades down there to keep you company!" Fanelli yelled into the void beyond the doorway.

"Cut the melodrama, Sergeant," Wentworth said, his face distorted in a sour expression.

"I'm just bullshitting," Fanelli laughed softly. "We can't toss grenades down there. They probably have innocent prisoners."

"What if they don't come out?" Wentworth whispered. "Do we lob a concussion grenade?"

"Hope we won't have to," Fanelli replied. "That'd be pretty rough on the prisoners, too. Probably survive, but they might not be thrilled about it—"

"Look!" a voice echoed from the basement. "We're comin' out! We don't have any guns, so don't shoot. Okay?"

"If we even think you're up to something we'll blow you away so fast you'll have friction burns on your ass," Fanelli warned.

"You have such a way with words," Wentworth sighed.

Three men emerged from the basement, their hands on their heads, fingers interlaced. One man carried a nightstick on his belt and all three had Nova stun guns clipped to their trousers.

"I want to see your hands on the sink and your legs a hundred miles apart," Wentworth ordered as he herded the trio across the room. "One of you tries to resist and I'll burn all three of you."

"You want to hold these suckers while I check out the basement?" Fanelli asked as he took the baton and stun guns from the hoodlums.

"There could be more of them down there," Wentworth warned. "Maybe you'd better wait until the captain gets back."

"What if he doesn't?" Fanelli asked.

"Unhappy thought," Wentworth frowned. "But you've got a point. Be careful down there."

"Sure thing, Lieutenant," Fanelli assured him as he moved toward the basement door.

Fanelli slowly descended the stairs, Uzi braced for action. The basement was drab and ugly, with gray stone walls and a concrete floor. Fanelli noticed a desk at the foot of the stairs. Handcuffs, leg irons, and nightsticks hung from nails in a cork board mounted on the wall. A coffee maker sat on a small table in a corner and the desk was littered with magazines and clipboards.

The basement proved to be very large, with two corridors extending from the guard station. The corridors were separated by a concrete divider eight feet wide. Fanelli carefully peered down both corridors, but saw no one.

"What's going on?" a female voice cried, confused and ragged.

"Maybe somebody's come to free us," another feminine voice said hopefully.

"Or they're killing the others!" a panicked male voice cried. "They're probably gunning down the others! They'll come for us next!"

Fanelli stepped into the corridor and moved toward the sound of the voices. He found six cells, each containing a teenage boy or girl. The average age of the prisoners appeared to be roughly nineteen, and none could be over twenty-one. All were naked standing within their concrete cages. The cells were only six feet wide in each direction. None of the cells had windows, toilets, or sinks. Each kid had been given two buckets, one containing water. The suffocating stench of excrement and urine in the air gave away what the other bucket was for.

Thin faces with bloodshot eyes stared back at Fanelli as he peered through the bars of the cell doors. The prisoners appeared to be half-starved. Their cheeks were hollow and ribs protruded beneath thinly padded skin. The young peoples' faces were bruised and dirty. Most of the girls had raw red marks on their necks and breasts.

It was hard to see in the poor light, but Fanelli swore he saw needle marks on the arms of virtually all the captives. Most also appeared to have small round burns on their ribs, thighs, and abdomens. The marks were spaced just the right distance to be the work of a stun gun employed for torture.

Fanelli found one young blond girl sitting on the edge of a cot. The girl raised her head to stare vacantly at him. Her nose had evidently been broken and bent out of shape. Dark bruises marked her cheeks and one eye was swollen shut. Her full lips were bruised and cut. Burn marks marred her breasts. One nipple had been charred black.

"No more, mister," she whispered helplessly. "Please, no more."

"No more," Fanelli assured her. "I promise you, no more."

He walked rigidly from the cellblock, his stomach knotted with anger and disgust. Fanelli's vision was blurred and he realized his eyes were filled with tears. He mounted the stairs to the kitchen above.

"Find anything?" Wentworth inquired as Fanelli approached.

"Yeah," Fanelli said with a hard nod. He glared at the three hoodlum guards. "Where are the keys to those cells, you scumbag piles of shit?"

"Hey, that ain't our fault," one of the thugs declared. He and the other two were still in a front-leaning rest position against the sink. They gazed over their shoulders at Fanelli and saw the expression of murderous fury on his face.

"Sure," Fanelli remarked as he gathered up two of the Nova stun guns that had been taken from the trio. "I bet they made you torture those kids, huh?"

He lunged suddenly at the first hoodlum, a stun gun in each fist. Fanelli jammed the metal probes into the guy's kidneys and pressed the buttons to both devices simultaneously. The goon's body jerked and arched backward, his mouth open in silent agony as his head bobbed with the twin charges of electricity.

"Joe!" Wentworth snapped. "That's enough!"

Fanelli removed the stun guns and the thug slumped to the floor, his body still twitching from the violent shock. The other hoods recoiled from Fanelli, their eyes wide with astonishment and fear. The angry merc still held the Nova stunners in his fists.

"Where are those fuckin' keys, damn it!" he demanded.

"For Chrissake!" one of the thugs replied. "They're in the goddamn desk!"

O'Neal and Caine entered the kitchen, roughly escorting

Bowers, the chemist they'd captured upstairs. The Hard Corps pair gazed down at the man Fanelli had stunned senseless.

"You guys having fun?" O'Neal inquired.

"You go down to the basement and see what these bastards have been up to and you'll want to string them up by their balls with piano wire!" Fanelli replied.

"I wouldn't be surprised," O'Neal admitted. "Mr. Bowers here has told us a lot about the drug crap these bastards have been up to. Haven't you, Bowers?"

"Don't be so proud of yourselves," the chemist snorted. "I don't know who you bastards are, but you'll never make this stick in court. Everything you got was by illegal force. You'll never get away with this—"

"We already have," O'Neal told him. "We'll leave you guys and make a phone call. When the police show up, they'll find lots of evidence waiting for them. Enough to arrest all you slime and shut down the Fellowship of Ultimate Living for keeps."

"And after the other kids here see what you've done to those poor fools locked in the cells downstairs, nobody will testify on your behalf," Fanelli added. "Narcotics, torture, kidnapping, and probably murder. You guys are all gonna take a hard fall."

"But we're just little fish," Bowers remarked. "Glover and Thor got away."

"Not really," O'Neal replied. "Well, since we've got some cells downstairs, let's let the prisoners out and lock these cretins in instead."

"That'll be fun," Fanelli leered. "I hope those kids have enough strength left to take out some of their frustrations on you sons of bitches before the cops arrive."

"Okay," William O'Neal announced. "Let's wrap things up here. We've still got a hell of a lot of work left to do before this job is finished."

CHAPTER 11

HAROLD GLOVER SAT behind a wide desk with a clear glass top. He was dressed in a white short-sleeved shirt and white shorts with matching knee socks and tennis shoes. The cult leader calmly sipped a Perrier as he smiled at the three men seated in the white leather chairs facing his desk.

"I hope you chaps had a nice flight," Glover remarked. "Or should I say flights? After all, you didn't arrive on the same plane. Did you?"

"It was satisfactory," Jean-Claude LeTrec assured him. "I just hope everything else will be as well."

The Frenchman returned Glover's smile, but the gesture seemed totally insincere. LeTrec looked like a sneaky little weasel with his slicked-back black hair and pencil-thin mustache, small dark eyes, and a narrow mean mouth. One can't judge a person by his appearance, even in LeTrec's case, because he was far worse than he appeared to be.

LeTrec was a freelance go-between for the Corsican Union and the Triad syndicates operating in Southeast Asia. LeTrec's grandfather had started the "family business" at the turn of the century, when most of Southeast Asia was still under French rule. The senior LeTrec had discovered the potential for considerable profit in the opium traffic of the Golden Triangle. Pierre LeTrec sold much of his opium to black marketeers in Western Europe, where it was converted into morphine. When the demand for the drug increased during World War I, LeTrec's Corsican connections sold most of their morphine to military sources on both sides of the conflict. Austrian, French, British, German, and American—the dope dealers sold to anyone willing to pay for the drug.

Another opium product had been developed in 1874 by a British chemist named C. R. Wright. Its scientific name was diacetylmorphine, but by 1900 it had become known throughout the world as heroin. By 1925 there were at least two hundred thousand heroin addicts in the United States alone. Organized crime had found a highly profitable addition to the drug trade and the LeTrec go-between operations blossomed in the process.

Jean-Claude's father, Pierre Gaston LeTrec, continued the Golden Triangle traffic through World War II. Much of this remained morphine sales to military buyers. In the 1960s, Jean-Claude became involved in his father's business as the Corsican Union in France formed an alliance with the Mafia, and heroin trafficking became more sophisticated. This was the so-called French Connection, but the poppy fields where most of the raw opium came from were still located in Turkey and the Golden Triangle.

Although the French had been driven out of Indochina, LeTrec continued to spend most of his time in Vietnam, Laos, and Cambodia, where he was welcomed by Triad syndicates among the ethnic Chinese communities. They also found a handsome profit by selling "scag" to American servicemen stationed in Vietnam. The power of the Triad expanded as the Chinese criminal network gained new footholds in England, Holland, the United States, and Canada. So Jean-Claude LeTrec was just carrying on the family business.

Harold Glover had dealt with LeTrec before. He didn't care much for the drug merchant, but he didn't have to like people to deal with them. LeTrec was a powerful and influential man, and as such was a valuable contact. That was all that mattered to Glover.

Kwan Li Que sat next to LeTrec. The middle-aged Chinese appeared to be a respectable businessman from Hong Kong or Taiwan. He wore a dark blue suit with a striped tie and black horn-rimmed glasses with an umbrella and briefcase on the floor near his feet.

In fact, this ordinary-looking man was a sub-chief of a Triad syndicate operating out of Singapore. The Singapore Triad was responsible for much of the drug traffic in Indonesia and the Malay archipelago. Kwan and Glover met shortly after the FUL was formed, and the men found their relationship to be mutually beneficial. Kwan stepped up his drug trade in Australia with Glover's help, and Glover's power in the region grew with help from Kwan.

Beyond this, Glover's white-slave trade kept Kwan supplied with an extremely valuable commodity in Southeast Asia. Kwan could sell the pick of Glover's women to brothels in Thailand, Malaysia, the Philippines, and even Singapore. LeTrec was more interested in using hollowed-out youngsters with broken spirits and American passports to act as mules for his heroin traffic, but Kwan enjoyed Glover's supply of girls as well.

The third man seated in front of Glover's desk was a well-muscled Japanese who listened a great deal and seldom spoke. Like most Japanese, he dressed in a neat, conservative manner, choosing to wear a light gray suit and a dark gray necktie. A long scar marked the left side of his cheek, from the corner of his eye to the jawline. It appeared to be a knife cut, yet it had actually been administered by a sword stroke. The man who'd given him the scar had died a split second later.

He had introduced himself as "Daiku," but none of the men in the office believed this was his real name. Daiku was sub-*oyabun* of a *yakuza,* or "Japanese Mafia," clan that had been quite successful dealing in gambling and prostitution in Osaka and was interested now in moving on to bigger and more ambitious endeavors. This included narcotics and white slavery, of course. Daiku had been sent to meet with Harold Glover to arrange for the merchandise for his clan's corrupt operations in Japan and abroad.

Glover was pleased with his visitors. Top representatives from three of the most powerful criminal organizations in the Orient, with influence that extended across the globe, had come to the cult leader's Australian headquarters because they wanted to do business with him. Glover wondered if the Golden Triangle Triad, the Singapore Triad, and the *yakuza* had ever attended a meeting together before.

"Is there some reason you feel you might be less than satisfied with either the arrangement or the merchandise, Mr. LeTrec?" Glover inquired, resting his elbows on the desktop.

"Things seem to have gone a little sour for your operation in California," LeTrec answered. "I received a cablegram about it at my hotel this morning."

"I also received word of this unfortunate incident, Harry," Kwan said quietly. "Does this have anything to do with your decision to meet with us ahead of schedule?"

"There is a connection," Glover admitted. It would be folly to lie to them. None of the gangsters were stupid and the evidence of a connection was obvious.

"You were forced to flee America?" Daiku inquired.

"I decided it would be wise for me to leave," Glover answered. "But I was not forced to do so in order to flee the police, if that's what you want to know, Mr. Daiku."

"Oh?" LeTrec raised his black eyebrows. "You left the United States two days ago, and at the same time your flight was leaving, your cult base in Northern California was being taken apart. I understand a number of your people in America are under arrest. Most of your employees you left behind are dead. Teenagers claim you kidnapped and tortured them. They claim they were forced to take drugs and the girls were raped by your men."

"The police found evidence, Harry," Kwan added.

"Lots of evidence. I'm afraid your cult may have to be dissolved soon. The Americans may want you extradicted. Interpol is probably looking for you already—and they know you're here in Australia."

"But they don't know where this base is located!" Glover replied, his eyes blazing. "By the time they find it, I'll be gone."

"Switzerland is rather nice this time of year," LeTrec commented. "And I believe you have some bank accounts there."

"Where I go and what I do aren't important," Glover replied icily. "All you need to know is that the security here remains solid. But you'll be leaving tomorrow anyway."

"And the merchandise leaves with us," Daiku stated.

"Now wait a minute, mate," the Australian began, a trace of concern slipping into his tone. "We're talking about transporting forty-two people to different parts of the world. I don't need to tell you, I assume, that that sort of thing has to be handled in a discreet manner."

"You're not in a very good position to declare terms, Harry," Kwan pointed out, impatient with Glover's attitude. He almost considered Glover a friend—almost. Glover was a manipulative opportunist and damn near a megalomaniac to boot, but Kwan had enjoyed a good working relationship with the Aussie. Still, business is business and Kwan's loyalty to the Triad always came first.

"Exactly what does that mean?" Glover asked with a frown.

"It means you're desperate," LeTrec answered. "You have to go into hiding and you have to do it soon. You also need money in a hurry."

"Your Fellowship of Ultimate Living has lost its credibility," Daiku added. "You can't return to America. You won't be able to set up the cult anywhere else because no one will trust you with young people again. Not after the incident in California becomes international news. You will have enough trouble simply finding a safe country to reside in."

"Of course you'll have to change your identity," Kwan told Glover. "Actually, you ought to come with me to Singapore. We can arrange for a very private cosmetic surgeon to give you a new . . . appearance. Perhaps even new fingerprints. I'm certain we can find a place for a man with your talents in the Triad."

"Maybe I can get you a job running a whorehouse in Thailand," LeTrec said with a cold smile. "Just don't bring along that muscle-bound Swedish ape. Thor Ornjarta is a sex criminal, still wanted in Western Europe for rape and murder. You should have gotten rid of that animal a long time ago."

"I'll take care of Thor," Glover assured him sharply. But the cult leader realized LeTrec had a valid point. The Swede was a liability. Now that the cult was falling apart, Thor was no longer useful. He would have to go. "So, what you gentlemen seem to be saying is I'm caught between a rock and a hard place and now you're going to squeeze me. Correct?"

"You have to sell your girls to our white slavery connections," Kwan stated. "And the other youths to our narcotics branch in order to serve as transporters of our products. You don't have time to find another market, Harry. You *have* to sell to us. You know that as well as we do."

"We already set a price," Glover reminded them. "Each one of you agreed to a price in advance."

"But circumstances have changed," Kwan hinted darkly.

"And so the price changes," LeTrec announced. "We'll buy your little children for half the previously agreed price."

"Whatever happened to the code of honor you fellows always claim is so bloody important to you?" Glover scowled.

"You never heard anything like that from me," LeTrec

told him. "It's a law of good business that when you have someone over a financial barrel, you take advantage of it."

"You are not *yakuza*, Mr. Glover," Daiku stated. The Japanese gangster seemed uncomfortable seated next to the two Triad representatives. Japanese and Chinese have never gotten along very well, and Daiku didn't seem to like LeTrec any better than he liked Kwan. "You shouldn't expect us to be too concerned about offending you because you obviously have no sense of honor. So why should you benefit from our code of honor when you do not grasp the concept in your own personal philosophy?"

"Oh?" Glover raised his eyebrows. A tone reminiscent of his speeches crept into his voice. "Am I such a villain because I lure pretty boys and beautiful girls into trouble? Am I so powerless when I make them completely obedient to me? Am I so alone when I get them softened up so you blokes can get your very interested hands all over them? Well, if that is the case, why do you do business with me? The answer is you're no better than I am. I wouldn't be in business if I didn't have people like you who buy what I can sell."

"You question my honor?" Daiku demanded, his back rigid as he sat up stiffly.

"No," Glover replied, eyes flashing. "You spat on mine. Let me remind you of something, Daiku-san or whoever the hell you really are. This is my home. You don't come in here and talk this crap to me. I'm in a tough position right now and everything you three said about me being forced to accept your terms is true. But I've been in worse scrapes before. And there's a limit to what I'll put up with in my own home."

"Let's calm down," Kwan urged.

"Each of you came here with three bodyguards," Glover continued. "Of course I insisted that none of them be armed while they're at my base. Now, I know your Triad enforcers out in the hallway are *kung fu* experts, and I know Daiku-san is a great swordsman and his three *kobun* bodyguards are probably skilled in karate and kendo. None of that crap will get very far up against a gun, and my people are packing lots of firepower. So if any of you would care to start a war at this base, I would be most happy to oblige."

"I don't like to be threatened," LeTrec warned.

"Neither do I," Glover said, spreading his arms in a forgiving gesture. "So I suggest we stop talking about things that are going to upset us and get back to business. You want the kids. Fine. I want to get rid of them. I also have close to a hundred kilos of heroin and I want to sell it, too. Would you care to buy your dope back, Li Que?"

"Not really," Kwan answered. "Do you want it, Monsieur LeTrec?"

"All right," the Frenchman agreed. "A hundred kilos?"

"We'll say ninety-five," Glover replied.

"One hundred thousand British pounds sterling," LeTrec announced with a smile.

"It's worth ten times that much," Glover responded, frowning.

"Not to me," LeTrec told him. "Take it or leave it."

"Sold," Glover said, aware that there was no point in arguing. "Now, most of the kids haven't been fully conditioned yet. I've got them happily docile and in complete obedience to my every word, but none of them have been forced to shoot up anything and the girls haven't gone through 'the process' yet."

"That's not what we agreed upon," Daiku said sternly.

"Neither is half-price," Glover answered. "Now don't worry. I picked this lot from my California harvest for two reasons. First, they're all small, young, easy to handle. Secondly, they're the *crème de la crème* of my harvest. The women are quite ravishing to look at, and the lads are totally obedient. I even had one of them kiss my shoes before breakfast every morning."

"Not much comfort in that," LeTrec muttered.

"Harry has to accept our terms and I don't think it will hurt us to accept his," Kwan remarked. "We have a deal, Harry."

"You and Mister Glover have a deal," Daiku stated. "You do not speak for the *yakuza*, Kwan-san."

"I didn't presume to do so," the Chinese assured the Japanese gangster. "I speak only for myself and the interests of my Triad."

"The Golden Triangle still comes out way ahead," Le-Trec decided. "You've got a deal, Harry."

"Reluctantly, I agree," Daiku announced. "But I am glad the *yakuza* will not be doing business with you again, Mr. Glover."

"I can live with that," Glover replied. "So let's discuss transportation and payment arrangements."

CHAPTER 12

THE HARD CORPS arrived in Australia less than six hours after Harold Glover and his group had deplaned at Sydney International. The mercenaries' forged passports and visas allowed them to pass through customs without a hitch. They brought along some camping gear, including tents, canteens, first-aid kits, olive-drab fatigue uniforms and boots, but no weapons except for Caine's survival knife and three Puma Bowie knives. There was nothing suspicious about some tourists planning to do some camping in the outback.

A large variety of vehicles was available at the Hertz and Avis offices at the airport. The mercs decided on renting a Chevy station wagon because it was the type of car that wouldn't attract much attention in most circumstances within city limits. The young woman at the counter was quite pleasant and assured them that they could leave their rental at another branch office in another city without extra charge, but mileage on the car would be another matter and traveling from city to city in Australia can take in a lot of miles.

"Oh," she added as she handed Wentworth the keys.

"Don't forget the traffic is on the left. I understand in America ya drive on the wrong side."

"That's sort of a matter of opinion," Wentworth replied, handing the keys to Fanelli. "The *left* side, right? Same as in England?"

"Actually," the woman answered, "it's the English drive on the same side as *we* do in Australia. That's nit-pickin', sir. Do enjoy yar holiday."

"Thanks very much," O'Neal told her.

"You're welcome," she said with a smile. "G'd day, sir."

They loaded their camping gear in the back of the station wagon and drove from the airport. Sydney is the largest city in Australia. It's also the largest city in an English-speaking Commonwealth nation outside of London, England. One-fifth of the entire population of Australia live in Sydney. Yet Sydney is remarkably different from big cities in the United States or Western Europe.

This difference didn't seem very great at first. Sydney is a harbor city with skyscrapers, towering office buildings, and huge apartment complexes. From a distance, Sydney vaguely resembles Miami, or even Chicago. Yet there is no haze or smog hovering over the city. The sky is brighter and cleaner than in most American cities.

And the biggest difference is the people. In most American or European cities with a population of more than three million people, driving a car is an exercise in controlling one's temper, honing one's reflexes, and occasionally confronting outright terror. However, Joe Fanelli soon noticed that being behind the wheel in Sydney was a different experience.

The Australian drivers seemed far more relaxed behind the wheel. They were more courteous and good-natured on the road. Although there were many vehicles in the streets, traffic moved smoothly without the traffic jams common in Los Angeles, or the maniacal speeding found in Rome or Brussels, or the ruthless "get out of my way" attitude of drivers in New York City.

The Hard Corps noticed that the Austrailians were mostly a very pleasant, good-natured, and amiable people. Harold Glover's smiling charm was a masquerade, but for most other Australians it seemed to be second nature. The Aussies also appeared to be very active. Outdoor sports are extremely popular in Australia. The country has one of the highest standards of living in the world and most Australians are well fed and well educated.

However, the Hard Corps hadn't come to Australia on a vacation. Although they found Australia far more appealing than Lebanon or Bolivia, they were still on a mission, and there was only one man in Sydney they needed to locate.

"Where the hell does this Basil hang out?" Fanelli asked as he drove the wagon into downtown Sydney and entered the business district at the intersection of Pitt and George Street.

"A place near King's Cross," O'Neal answered as he checked a small notepad to be certain of the information. "It's called *The Drunken Cockatoo*."

"Oh, God," Wentworth muttered. "Sounds like another classy establishment where one can find the lowest lifeforms that still qualify as species *homo sapiens*."

"You mean it's a gay bar?" Fanelli inquired.

"No," the lieutenant said with a sigh. "But I think you ought to sue every school you went to in New Jersey for failure to provide you with a decent education. Then again, they may have done the best they could with what they had to work with."

"They had blackboards and chalk," Fanelli replied. "What they teach you at those fancy private schools down South, Lieutenant? How to expectorate instead of spit?"

"Pay attention to the road, Joe," O'Neal ordered. "We don't have time to get lost while we're looking for this drunk cockatoo hangout."

"We're going the right way, sir," Steve Caine assured the Hard Corps commander as he consulted a street map of the city. "We'll find it."

"I hope Basil can be of help to us," Wentworth remarked. "The information McShayne had doesn't sound very encouraging."

"Nobody else sounded any better," O'Neal reminded him.

The Hard Corps needed two things before they could continue their mission in Australia. They had to get their hands on some weapons with adequate firepower and they had to locate the headquarters of the Fellowship of Ultimate Living. Waldo Basil might be able to help them with both needs.

According to the data John McShayne had compiled for the Hard Corps with the computers back at the compound, Basil was a thirty-seven-year-old veteran of the Vietnam War. He had been born somewhere in the hills of Kentucky and probably never had a pair of boots until he enlisted at the age of seventeen. Basil had wound up as a truck driver and general clerk for a supply section in Saigon, but later became a unit armor at Danang. Although he didn't have a combat MOS, Basil frequently complained to his CO that he wanted to get involved in the action and eventually decided to do it by himself.

Basil stole a jeep, loaded it up with an M-60 machine gun, a couple of M-16s, grenade launchers, and plenty of ammo. Then he simply drove off into the bush to hunt Vietcong. He found some and killed nine enemy troops before one of them managed to put two AK rounds in the crazy Kentucky boy. The U.S. Army wasn't quite sure what to do with Basil after the incident. They didn't know if they should give him a medal or court-martial him. The Army wound up giving him a Bronze Star and a Purple Heart and sending him back to the States.

Basil wanted to return to Vietnam, but Uncle Sam didn't want him there. The guy was a potential threat to other American soldiers because of his irrational behavior and probably should have been quietly discharged with a "medical" under honorable conditions. Instead, the Army

kept him, and Basil got involved in the black market trade
with civilians.

When the CID caught him, Basil's war record saved
him from Leavenworth, and the Army bounced him out
with a Section Eight. Needless to say, when the Army
thinks you're too crazy to keep you, not many civilian employers want to hire you. Basil couldn't hold a job and had
long periods of unemployment—at least officially. He
probably didn't declare his income to the IRS from fencing
stolen goods and dealing in black market goods.

Eventually, Basil was arrested for receiving stolen
M-16s supplied by a couple of idiots stationed at Fort
Knox. Basil managed to get out on bail and fled the country before he could stand trial. Somehow, for reasons
known best to Basil himself, the guy wound up in Australia.

Basil had become a successful gunrunner in the land
down under. Both the Sydney Police and the Australian
branch of Interpol had brought him in for questioning on
several cases involving illegal firearms, but they could
never get enough evidence to make an arrest. Nonetheless,
Basil appeared to be one of the biggest arms dealers in the
country and apparently he'd finally acquired enough savvy
to keep his ass out of jail.

O'Neal understood Wentworth's apprehensions about
Basil. In fact, he shared the lieutenant's doubts that Basil
was reliable or even rational. However, they needed
weapons and information, and Basil was their best bet to
find both.

Fanelli drove the Chevy wagon into King's Cross. The
streets were lined with theaters, taverns, massage parlors,
and nightclubs. The caliber of these establishments varied
to suit a wide range of tastes and expense accounts. Some
places were expensive and well kept, even respectable.
Others looked run-down, cheap, and probably shady.

Not surprisingly, The Drunken Cockatoo fit the latter
category. One could easily miss the little tavern, sand-

wiched between a diner and an X-rated movie theater. A dark green shade was drawn over the dirty window at the front of the bar, but an OPEN sign was pressed against the glass. A board had been nailed above the door and bore the name of the establishment. Fanelli parked at the curb.

"This place could give dumps a bad name," Fanelli muttered as he switched off the engine.

"For once we're in agreement," Wentworth said dryly.

"Come on," O'Neal growled as he opened a door. "We haven't even gone inside yet."

"Somehow I don't think that'll change anyone's opinion, sir," Caine commented, following the others to the door.

He was right. The furniture in The Drunken Cockatoo looked like it belonged in a trash heap. A glassy-eyed bartender with a nose that resembled a red doorknob leaned on the plywood counter, sipping a large mug of beer and reading a cheap tabloid newspaper. Two middle-aged men dressed in shabby torn clothes were seated at a table across the room. They were getting drunk with a woman who had bright orange hair, gray at the roots. The men were taking turns groping at her under the table.

"Oh?" The bartender looked up at the four strangers with surprise. "G'd day, gents. What'll it be? Beer or whiskey? Wouldn't touch the wine, if I was you. Bloody awful, it is. Local stuff, ya know."

"They're drinking wine," Fanelli said, indicating the two men with the orange-haired woman.

"Gawd, mate!" The bartender glared at Fanelli. "Don't want'a wind up like *them,* d'ya?"

"We want to see Basil," O'Neal said, coming straight to the point and placing a twenty-dollar bill on the counter.

"Basil?" The bartender frowned, but he stared down at the money with interest. "Seems to me I used to know a bloke by that name, but my memory ain't so good these days . . ."

"You don't get any more money unless you help us find

Basil," O'Neal declared in a gruff voice. "We're not cops and we don't want to hurt him. Just need to talk to him."

"Wait a minute, mate," the barman insisted, grabbing up the twenty. "I jus' remembered that I got this lad what works for me. He's in the back room. Now, he used to talk to Basil quite a bit there. I'll go have a chat with him and see what he can tell me. All right?"

"Make it a short chat," O'Neal replied.

The bartender opened a door behind the bar and stepped into the back room. Muffled voices reached beyond the closed door, but the Hard Corps couldn't understand a word. The bartender appeared thirty seconds later.

"The boy says he can contact Basil," the barman announced as he leaned on the counter. "You blokes are Yanks, too, ain't ya? Knew ol' Basil back in the States, did you?"

"No," O'Neal answered, taking another twenty from his wallet. "When do we meet with Basil?"

"Maybe you don't," a man announced as he stepped from the back room.

He was thin and pale with a bald, egg-shaped head. A hawkish nose jutted between hooded dark eyes and his mouth resembled a deep knife slash. The bald man wore an OD T-shirt, baggy field pants, and a pair of dog tags hanging from a thick chain around his neck, which resembled an oversized choker collar for a dog. A MAC-10 machine pistol hung from a shoulder strap near his right hip.

"I don't think Basil knows you guys," he declared, a trace of a backwoods twang in his voice. "I ain't so sure he'd want to know y'all."

"Think Basil would like to know this little green guy?" O'Neal asked as he tossed a fifty-dollar American bill on the counter.

"Well now." The bald man smiled. "Reckon everybody likes little green pictures of President Grant. I kinda like to collect these myself. Y'all got anymore?"

"You're Basil?" O'Neal asked.

"That's what the dog tags say," the bald man said as he

jingled the metal disks that hung from his neck. "Now what you boys want?"

"Private conversation," O'Neal replied, jerking his head toward the two men with the orange-haired woman.

"Hank." Basil turned to the bartender. "Get those loafers outa here and close shop for a while."

"Okay," the barman replied. He stepped from behind the bar and stomped toward the trio across the room. "Hey, ya bleedin' perverts! What th'hell ya doin'?"

"What got yar arse, mate?" one of the drunks demanded in a slurred voice.

"I don't appreciate ya diddlin' about with that damn tart ya drug in here," Hank snapped. "This here's a respectable place, not a bloody whorehouse."

"Piss off, ya prude arsehole," the woman spat. "Girl's gotta earn a livin', don't she?"

"Not in my pub ya don't," Hank replied. He grabbed both men by the nape of the neck and yanked them out of their chairs. "Now get outa here and take this gutter slut with ya."

"Oh, fuck," one of the drunks complained. "Ya sure know how to ruin a mood, Hank!"

"Go on, ya louts!" the bartender snarled as he dragged the pair to the door. "Get outa here!"

"We're goin', ya batty sod!" the woman muttered, following her male companions out the door.

"And don't come back for at least two hours!" Hank added.

"Okay," one of the drunks replied. "See ya later."

"Right," Hank said as he watched them stagger up the street. "The next round'll be on the house."

Hank shut the door and bolted it. He reversed the sign in the window to let others know the place was closed for business. Wentworth stared at the bartender with astonishment.

"You have a curious relationship with your customers," the Hard Corps lieutenant remarked.

"Oh, they know I'm not really mad at 'em," Hank said

with a shrug. "Ya don't hold a grudge 'bout little shit like that."

"Hank's my partner," Basil explained as he poured himself a shot of whiskey. "I vouch for him. Now, let's get to business."

"We need some weapons," O'Neal explained. "I understand you're the man to talk to."

"How'd ya find out about me?" Basil asked suspiciously, still holding on to the Ingram machine pistol.

"Friends of friends," O'Neal answered. "Look, we're buyers. Don't need a lot. Two rifles, automatic assault rifles with Starlite scopes if you have them. Two submachine guns, nine-millimeter parabellum. Four handguns, either nine-mill or forty-five-caliber."

"And explosives," Fanelli added. "Hand grenades and plastic explosives. Composition-4 or something like that. Only need about two pounds, plus detonators, blasting caps, maybe some primacord."

"I might be able to get what you want," Basil told them. He placed a hardcover notebook on the counter. "Take a look at my catalog. Now some of that stuff might take a couple of months to deliver..."

"We need the guns tonight," O'Neal answered as he opened the book and glanced over two pages of military handguns.

"*Tonight?*" Basil glared at him. "I'm not running a McDonald's here."

"I think the Browning nine-millimeter might be a better choice than a forty-five Colt under the circumstances," Wentworth said as he glanced over O'Neal's shoulder. "Ammunition would be the same caliber as the ammo for the submachine guns."

"I can get the Brownings for you tonight," Basil explained. "There are a lot of them in Australia because the Browning is the standard side arm for the military here. Can't say I can get y'all everything you want on such short notice, though."

"Okay." O'Neal examined the submachine gun choices. "You have Uzis in stock?"

"Not right now," Basil sighed. "Sure wish I did. Real popular item. Right now I've got some of these MAC-10s. Nice little room-cleaner."

"We're familiar with the Ingram," O'Neal stated. "Might be okay if you only want to deliver a very fast salvo at opponents at extremely close range, but the Ingram isn't a practical combat weapon. The barrel is too short, accuracy sucks, and the rate of fire is close to a thousand rounds per minute. You burn up a thirty-two-round mag too damn fast. The MAC-10 might look good in movies, but it isn't that good in actual combat."

"I know," Caine added. "I used one a while back. If I have to be more than ten yards from an opponent, I'd rather use a bow and arrow."

"Well, I've got some Aussie F-1 submachine guns," Basil declared. "You boys probably never fired one of 'em before. Kinda like the British Patchett submachine gun. Looks kinda like a two-foot piece of pipe with a walnut buttstock attached at one end with a pistol grip near the middle. See the picture of it?"

"Yeah," O'Neal said with a nod. Basil's description was pretty accurate. "It uses a top-loading magazine?"

"Looks kinda weird, don't it?" Basil laughed. "Not a real accurate weapon, but it's better than the Ingram for accuracy and distance. The picture makes it look like the magazine is blocking the front sight, but actually the front sight is located at the side of the magazine well. See? Take a good look. Better control than with the Ingram, too. Fires six hundred rounds per minute. Barrel's longer, too, so ya got more range."

"What is it?" Wentworth asked. "Selective fire or full-auto only?"

"Full-auto only," Basil answered. "Blowback action and uses a thirty-four round mag. 'Course, it's nine-millimeter parabellum. You want 'em?"

"You can have them for us tonight?" O'Neal asked.

"I can give you four F-1 subs and the four Brownings tonight," Basil confirmed. "That's no problem, but I can't get you no assault rifles until the middle of the week. If you'd been here two days ago I could have gotten you a couple of FALs, but I sold 'em all to a New Zealand outfit that's smugglin' arms to some Cambodians fightin' the Vietnamese in Southeast Asia. Gawd, I was glad to do business with those boys. Hope they kick fuckin' Charlie's ass."

"Sounds good to me, too," O'Neal assured him.

"You was in-country too, huh?" Basil grinned. "Fuckin' 'Nam seems like yesterday, don't it?"

"I think we all carry some of it around with us," O'Neal answered. "We'll need about a thousand rounds of ammunition."

"You boys are serious," the gunrunner remarked. "No problem there. I can give you a thousand rounds of regular NATO rounds, one-hundred-fifteen-grain full-jacketed parabellums. Sorry, but I don't have any hollow-points or Glaser safety rounds."

"That's okay," O'Neal said. "Extra magazines included?"

"Four mags for each weapon," Basil said with a nod. "Now, you said you wanted some grenades and plastique. I don't have much in stock right now. Got maybe a dozen SAS 'flash-bang' grenades from England. Kinda concussion grenade, right? Don't have any C-4, but I do have about one pound of C-3. Familiar with it?"

"Yeah," Fanelli said without enthusiasm. "It's not as powerful as C-4, it's sort of oily, and it can throw out toxic fumes if you use a lot of it in a confined space. That shouldn't be a problem with just a pound of the stuff."

"Okay," Basil said as he placed a pocket calculator on the bar. "Let me add this all up and I'll tell ya what y'all gotta pay for this stuff. Ya know, those F-1 choppers usually sell for five hundred Australian dollars—and that's more than five hundred American, you know. But, I reckon we're all veterans of the same war and all, so I'll lower the price a bit to four-fifty American dollars for each piece."

"That's very generous," O'Neal told him.

"Let's see," Basil commented as he finished punching the keys to his calculator. "That'll be four thousand and five hundred dollars for the whole shitload. Half now and half on delivery. Fair enough?"

"Sure," O'Neal agreed. "Now there's one other matter we need to discuss. What do you know about Harold Glover and the Fellowship of Ultimate Living?"

"Oh, Gawd," Basil snorted, shaking his head. "Don't tell me y'all plan to get mixed up with that fuckin' cult? Besides, I hear they do their own recruitin' and they don't hire ya just cause ya show up with yore own guns."

"We don't plan to work for the cult, exactly," O'Neal explained. "Actually, we just want to find where the headquarters is located. Now, we figure Glover's got armed personnel there. They wouldn't get their weapons from a legal gun shop. That means they're probably buying from an arms merchant like yourself. You're supposed to be the biggest gunrunner in Sydney."

"Oh, shit no," Basil replied, though it was clear he liked the compliment. "There's other boys in this racket who deal a lot more than I could ever begin to. Native Aussies mostly. You know, Aussies generally like Americans, but a lot of folks still like to do business with the local boys. Figure I might be CIA or somethin'. Ain't that a funny one! *Me* CIA? Don't even know what it stands for."

"Then you don't have any idea where the cult base is?" O'Neal said, disappointed.

"I didn't say that exactly," Basil said with a sly smile. "Ya see, a buddy of mine . . . well, more what ya'd call an o'sociate, was runnin' a big-time arms-dealin' business down in Melbourne. For future reference, that's a better city for gunrunnin' than Sydney. Anyways, this ol' boy got his ass in a crack with the po-lice. Turned out he was sellin' guns to some would-be terrorist revolutionary outfit in Tasmania who wanted to make the island a separate coun-

try under a Marxist or neo-Nazi government or somethin'
like that. Can't recall the exact details offhand, but the
cops was hot on the guy's ass."

"What's that have to do with Glover and the FUL?"
O'Neal asked, trying to cut the gunrunner off before the
story got too long.

"Why hell, the guy in Melbourne was sellin' guns to the
cult," Basil explained as if this should have been obvious.
"So he comes to me and says he needs some favors from
me. Wants my help in gettin' the fuck outa the country
'cause I know some pilots who can fly you to New Zealand
and set y'all up with folks who'll help ya find a safe hidin'
place for a while. He needs all his money for runnin', so
instead of payin' me exactly, he offers to give me his
clients instead. Not a bad deal, so I took it. He gave me the
addresses, so to speak. Well, I'm a might fussy 'bout who I
do business with. I don't like Glover and his outfit, so I
just never contacted 'em. Done some business with a few
of the other clients the Melbourne boy told me about, but I
steered clear of the FUL. 'Course, Glover was gettin' guns
from other dealers anyway, so I imagine it never mattered
much to him that the guy high-tailed it outa the country—"

"Come on, Basil," O'Neal urged. "Do you know where
the cult base is? Yes or no, damn it!"

"Shit, yeah." Basil smiled. "Y'all never throw away
potentially valuable information in my line of work. Never
know when it might come in useful."

"We'll pay for that information, Basil," O'Neal declared.

"How much do you have in mind?" the gunrunner inquired. "I mean, I've been sittin' on this information for
almost a year now. Figured it might be somethin' I can use
to make a deal with the cops if'n my butt ever winds up in
a legal sling."

"It won't be any use for that purpose in another day or
two," O'Neal told him. "Did you hear about what happened to the California branch of the cult two days ago?"

"Must not have made the headlines here," Basil answered.

"I read 'bout it," Hank the bartender interrupted. "Place got busted for drugs, kidnappin', torturin' kids. Really dirty stuff. These blokes are tellin' you the truth, Basil. Glover's back in Australia and the cops are lookin' for him already. That cult's on the run."

"Not such good news for me financially." Basil frowned. "But it'll sure be nice to get rid of Glover and his lot. Wait a second. Y'all plannin' to hit those bastards? I'll be damned. The four of you intend to attack the FUL alone? Man, that's a lot of trouble to go to in order to commit suicide. Even if they're on the run, they gotta be goddamned dangerous."

"That's our business," O'Neal told him. "How about five hundred for the location of the FUL headquarters?"

"Better than nothin' and that's what I'll have otherwise," Basil replied. "I'd better get the map with the base marked on it. Have it locked away in my safe . . . say, just thought of somethin'. The damn place is in South Australia. That's a far distance from here."

"I thought Sydney was in southern Australia," Fanelli remarked, recalling a map of the country he'd seen before they arrived in Australia.

"This is the south*east* part of Australia," Basil confirmed. "But South Australia is a different state."

"Ya see, we've got separate states here in Australia just like you Yanks got fifty states in the U.S.," Hank explained. "In Australia, we've only got six states and two mainland territories, plus the island dependencies, of course. Now, we're in New South Wales and the state of South Australia is to the west of us."

"Yeah," Basil added. "But don't forget New South Wales is bigger than Texas and South Australia's even larger. Australia is nearly as big as the United States, an' we got plenty of wide-open spaces here 'cause we've got only about one-fifteenth the population you've got in the States. The outback makes the Alaskan wilderness look

like a state park. It's no wonder the authorities haven't
been able to keep tabs on the FUL. Tryin' to keep track of
anything in the outback is a pain in the ass just 'cause of
the sheer size of it."

"So even with the map we'll have trouble locating the
base," Wentworth said with a nod. "I hope you have a
suggestion that might help, Basil."

"Why, 'course I do," the gunrunner replied cheerfully.
"Told you I've got some pilot friends. I can set you up with
somebody who'll fly you right to the base. 'Course you'll
probably wanna land close, but not too close, and there
might not be a decent runway around. No problem. Kip's a
smuggler, 'mong other things. He can land a 747 on a
bicycle lane if'n he has to."

"How much is this gonna cost us?" O'Neal asked.

"Shit," the gunrunner grinned. "I'll set y'all up with Kip
for free. After all, we've all been in Nam. Besides, you
boys might wanna do business with me again, if'n I treat
you right. Unless y'all get yoreselves killed, of course.
Hate to say it, but that's a real powerful possibility."

CHAPTER 13

Kɪᴘ McGʀᴇɢᴇʀ ᴏᴡɴᴇᴅ a "private airline service" at a small airstrip about two miles north of Botany Bay. The Hard Corps arrived at the airfield at nine-thirty that night. Waldo Basil was waiting for them. The bald little gunrunner may have been a little crazy and more than a little weird, but he was also a stand-up guy. The weapons were inside a hangar, waiting for the Hard Corps to inspect their order.

The F-1 submachine guns and Browning pistols were in excellent condition. Basil delivered everything he'd agreed to. The 9-mm ammunition, SAS grenades, and C-3 plastic explosives were all ready for the mercenaries. William O'Neal gave Basil the rest of his payment.

"Pleasure doin' business with you boys," the gunrunner said with a smile as he pocketed the money. He didn't bother to count it. He also figured the Hard Corps were stand-up guys as well. "Let me introduce y'all to Kip."

Basil approached a tall man dressed in a leather jacket with a fedora hat jammed on his tawny head. The guy also had a ten-day-old beard. The Hard Corps wouldn't have

149

been surprised if the theme from *Raiders of the Lost Ark* had come up from a cassette player in the background.

"G'd day, gents," Kip announced, revealing even white teeth as he shook hands with each of the mercs in turn. "I'm Kip McGreger, bush pilot and adventurer, at your service."

"Pleased to meet you," O'Neal told him. "Are you sure you can find the place we're looking for?"

"Hell yes," Kip confirmed. "I've been to parts of the outback even the kangaroos don't know about yet. Now, this cult base you're lookin' for is to the north of South Australia. Almost to the bloody Northern Territory. Be glad the base isn't up there."

"The Northern Territory is almost as big as Alaska," Basil explained.

"I'll try to remember that if it ever comes up on a TV quiz show," Fanelli muttered, getting a little tired of hearing about how big everything was supposed to be in Australia. It was like listening to a bunch of Texans.

"Are you sure your airplane is big enough to handle all of us?" O'Neal asked Kip.

"No problem at all," the bush pilot assured him. "She's an American-made C-130. Familiar with her? Used some of 'em in Vietnam for transportin' troops."

"Yeah," O'Neal confirmed. "I've logged more than eight hundred hours flying C-130s."

"That's great," Kip announced. "Then I've got me a co-pilot as well. Well, mates, if we're gonna hit those bastards by dawn, we'd best get movin', eh?"

The Hard Corps carried their supplies to the airplane. Kip climbed into the cockpit as the mercenaries loaded everything on board. The C-130 was indeed large enough for the four mercs, and there'd be enough room to bring back any kids they might rescue from the cult as well.

"Bill," James Wentworth began as he pulled O'Neal away from the others. "Do you mind if I make an observation?"

"Go ahead," the Hard Corps commander assured him.

"The parents group headed by the charming Ms. Henderson paid us only ten thousand dollars when they hired us," Wentworth began. "Since then, we've had to pay for rather expensive forged passports and other documents, tickets for Qantas to fly us to Australia, and Basil's five thousand dollars. And now Kip is being paid another four grand and that's not including the costs of ammunition, travel expenses, and what-have-you that we spent when we started this mission."

"Your point is we haven't made a profit so far with this mission," O'Neal replied with a sigh.

"Profit?" Wentworth rolled his eyes. "We haven't even broke even. We *are* mercenaries, after all. We're supposed to make some money doing this sort of thing. Those parents may never get around to paying us the forty grand they still owe us."

"We'll worry about that later," O'Neal told him.

"I know this mission has become sort of a personal crusade for you, Bill," Wentworth stated. "God knows it's worthwhile and I'm glad we took the mission."

"You don't sound very glad, Jim," O'Neal replied.

"I'm just saying if we're going to keep the Hard Corps in business we can't take on heartfelt missions that we have to pay for with our own money," Wentworth insisted. "And you know that as well as I do."

"I kind of forgot this time," O'Neal said with a weak smile. "But your point is well noted. Now, can we get in the plane so we can wrap this mission up?"

"The sooner the better," Wentworth assured him.

They boarded the plane. Wentworth joined Fanelli and Caine in the cargo section where the two merc sergeants were busy loading magazines with 9-mm cartridges. O'Neal joined Kip in the cockpit and waved at Basil as the gunrunner watched the plane prepare to taxi along the runway. O'Neal noticed a thick coil of black twisted leather on the floorboards near the rudder controls.

"Oh," he said, trying to stifle a chuckle. "I see you have a bullwhip, Kip. Use it for your adventures?"

"Always take it along in the outback, mate," the pilot replied. "Have it in case I come across any snakes."

"Snakes?" O'Neal raised his eyebrows.

"We've got more than a hundred species of poisonous snakes native to Australia!" Kip said above the drone of the warming engines. "More than any country in the world. We've also got the most deadly venomous snakes in the world. Saipan, death adder, and—the worst of the lot— the Australia tiger snake! Remember to watch out for those crawly critters when we reach the outback!"

"I'll remember!" O'Neal assured him. "But I'm more worried about snakes that walk on two legs and can shoot back at me!"

The Hard Corps didn't get to see much of the fabled outback from the air as the plane flew through the night sky. The ground below seemed mostly barren with an occasional patch of grass or eucalyptus tree. The flight continued for hours and the view from the windows of the C-130 didn't seem to change much.

"I saw an animal move down there," Fanelli remarked as he gazed out a window. "Looked like a small deer or maybe a dog of some kind."

"Could be a dingo," Caine commented without much interest. "The dingo is a nocturnal hunter and resembles a dog. It's supposed to have a pitiful howl, but it doesn't bark."

"God," Wentworth groaned. "Next we'll be discussing the mating habits of koala bears. Hey, Kip! How much longer before we reach our destination?"

"Any minute now!" the Aussie pilot replied as he had several times before.

"I hope we find it soon," O'Neal told Kip. The Hard Corps leader noticed the sky was lighter and the dawn sun would soon appear.

"Wishes can come true, mate," Kip announced as he pointed at a group of buildings below. "I think we found it."

O'Neal trained a pair of binoculars on the site. It resembled the Fellowship of Ultimate Living base the Hard Corps had raided in Northern California. Three wooden billets had been built, no doubt as quarters for the kids who had naively joined the cult.

The main house was obviously Glover's headquarters. It was a large two-story structure with a wide flat roof equipped with solar panels to tap the sun's energy for electricity. O'Neal couldn't tell much else about the place from the air, but the site was better protected than the previous FUL base.

Glover hadn't bothered to build a fence around the base. The vastness of the outback itself made escape unlikely. The site was also patroled by two Jeeps that circled the enemy compound like mechanical sharks waiting for something to kill. The area was almost twice as large as the Californian base and included a small lake and a helicopter pad.

Five other vehicles were parked at the rear of the big house. Two were extra Jeeps, two were dark-green buses, and the last vehicle was a truck. A guard walked foot patrol in the motor pool. O'Neal swung the binoculars back to the 'copter pad. Three choppers were parked on the five-acre clearing. The mercenary leader couldn't identify the type of 'copters due to the darkness, but each whirlybird was large enough to carry a dozen men.

O'Neal wondered how many opponents were inside the house. The enemy would certainly outnumber the Hard Corps, but the mercs were accustomed to fighting against bad odds. However, they weren't used to fighting with unfamiliar weapons. None of them had ever handled an F-1 submachine gun before or any weapon similar to it.

Well, it was too late to change their minds about the mission. It was also too late to elevate the plane to fly high enough to avoid attracting the attention of the enemy guards below. Kip had flown low in order to search the outback for the base. He had hoped to locate it in time to climb higher in the sky, but the plane was still suspiciously

low as it passed over the enemy compound. The patrol
vehicles stopped and guards craned their necks to stare up
at the C-130.

"Shit," O'Neal rasped. "They've made us."

"Maybe not," Kip replied, but the tone of his voice
didn't sound as if he was convinced of this. "They're not
expectin' any trouble, are they? Lots of planes fly over the
outback all the time. Only way to get from one place to
another in a hurry. Especially since there aren't any roads
through much of the outback . . ."

"They've made us," O'Neal repeated. "This is going to
be even tougher than we figured it would be."

"Captain?" Wentworth announced as he appeared at the
cockpit. "Perhaps you didn't notice, but our luck has just
turned bad."

"Kip and I were discussing that," O'Neal assured him.
"Seems to me we've got two choices and neither of them
are very good."

"Actually we've got four choices of action," Wentworth
corrected. "But I suspect you've already canceled out two
of them."

"We're not turning back and we're not heading for the
nearest safe airfield and coming back here tomorrow
night," O'Neal declared.

"That's what I thought," Wentworth said with a nod.

"What the hell's wrong with comin' back tomorrow?"
Kip demanded, glancing from the controls to O'Neal and
Wentworth. "You blokes have to finish this mission to meet
some sorta deadline or somethin'?"

"Glover isn't gong to stay put long," O'Neal answered.
"The son of a bitch must still be there right now. All those
helicopters and vehicles suggest he's getting ready to liqui-
date his assets and flee the country. Those assets include
the kids he conned into joining his cult. I wouldn't be surprised if he's got some buyers down there. Drug traffickers
and white slavers."

"Triad," Wentworth added. "That's what Saintly told
us."

"The bloody Triad is involved in this?" Kip glared at O'Neal. "Ya didn't bother to mention that!"

"Don't worry," O'Neal assured him. "You're just flying the taxi. We'll have to find a place to land. Somewhere far enough from here so the bad guys won't see you descend. Then you let us out and haul ass. We'll just have to play it by ear from there."

"Christ!" Kip muttered. "Sun will be up in ten minutes. You can't go chargin' in there in broad daylight. This is the bleedin' outback and a goddamn desert area at that. The bloody lake down there is manmade. You don't see any trees or bushes around here, do you? It's flat terrain and they'll see you comin' miles before you can reach this place. Bloody suicide."

"There's another way," O'Neal began. "But it'll mean more risk for you, Kip."

"Do I get a bonus for riskin' my arse?" the pilot asked slyly.

"How about two grand?" O'Neal replied. "You'll have to trust me to send you the money after we get back to the States. I'm a little low on cash right now."

"I reckon you're good for it," Kip said with a nod. "What the hell. Tell me what you want me to do."

CHAPTER 14

THE C-130 DESCENDED as the sun appeared in the pale morning sky. The guards on patrol within the Fellowship of Ultimate Living compound watched the plane descend behind a ridge about a quarter of a mile from the house. The FUL hired thugs were familiar with the area and realized the long stretch of flat prairie beyond the ridge could serve as a landing strip for the mysterious aircraft.

The two Jeeps on roving patrol headed toward the ridge while other FUL flunkies reported the news to their superiors inside the house. Some were ordered to the motor pool to get the other Jeeps. Two hoods were sent to one of the helicopters, carrying a light machine gun complete with bipod.

The C-130 rolled to a halt along the improvised runway as the first patrol Jeeps reached the ridge. Each vehicle contained two men, a driver and a partner armed with an FAL assault rifle with a Bushnell scope. One Jeep rolled over the ridge and headed down toward the plane while the driver of the second vehicle parked at the ridge and both men stepped from the ridge. They assumed position at the

summit, weapons aimed at the C-130 to cover the other
guards who approached the aircraft.

"G'd day!" Fanelli shouted to the approaching Jeep as
he emerged from the hold of the C-130 and waved cheerfully at the enemy gunmen. "Lookin' for shrimp for the
barbie?"

"Freeze, you Yank fuck!" the man riding shotgun in the
Jeep snarled as he pointed his FAL at Fanelli.

The Jeep came to a halt and the driver drew a revolver
from a shoulder-holster rig. Fanelli stood outside the plane
with his hands raised to shoulder level. The mercenary
didn't carry any weapon except a Puma knife in a belt
sheath at his hip.

"Jesus!" Fanelli exclaimed. "Watch where you're pointing that thing. Somebody could get hurt. Probably me."

"Hurt, hell!" the driver sneered. "You could be dead!"

"Wait a minute!" Fanelli began. "Didn't the pilot get
permission to land? Is that what this is about?"

"Shut up!" the rifleman ordered.

Kip McGregor opened the door to the cockpit and
leaned outside. "Hey, what the hell are ya doin' wavin'
those guns about?" he demanded.

"Get out of that fuckin' plane!" the driver ordered,
swinging his revolver toward Kip. "And no funny business. Me mates got ya covered so it ain't just us what's got
the drop on ya."

"Okay," Kip replied. "Just take it easy, mate. I'm just a
freelance pilot with a bit of engine trouble—"

"Move, damn it!" the guy with the pistol snarled.

William O'Neal slid open a trapdoor to the roof above
the cockpit and stood up on the seat, preparing to climb
through the opening with an F-1 submachine gun in his
fist. He assumed Wentworth and Caine were also in position at the rear emergency exit and a window by the right
wing.

"Down!" O'Neal hissed loud enough for Kip to hear the
command.

The pilot immediately ducked back inside the cockpit

and dropped to the floor. Fanelli had been watching Kip for the signal and immediately dropped to the ground and rolled under the plane. The gunmen at the Jeep fired their weapons too late. The pistol barked and fired a .38 slug into the metal skin of the plane at the threshold of the cockpit. The other hood's FAL spat a three-round burst into the ground, scant inches from Fanelli's rolling form.

O'Neal fired his F-1 from the roof of the C-130 and sprayed the enemy Jeep with 9-mm parabellums. The two gunmen cried out as high-velocity bullets tore into their torsos. Their bodies tumbled out of the vehicle and fell lifeless to the ground.

The two gunmen who'd remained up at the ridge were startled by the unexpected gunfire from the roof of the plane. They had aimed their weapons at Fanelli and Kip, but tried to swing the FAL assault rifles toward O'Neal's position. They didn't see James Wentworth, who had climbed from the emergency exit and stationed himself under the tail of the C-130.

Wentworth fired his F-1 blaster at the ridge, tilting the unfamiliar weapon upward and peering through the oddly aligned sights. Two 9-mm slugs kicked dirt from the lip of the ridge. Others sizzled harmlessly through air near the gunmen. Three bullets smashed into the face and neck of an enemy rifleman in a prone position at the ridge.

The other FUL gunman was understandably alarmed when his partner suddenly flopped about with a crimson pulp where his face had formerly been. The survivor didn't watch the completion of his comrade's death throes. He rolled away from the ridge and scrambled for the cover of the Jeep. Steve Caine had climbed onto the wing at the opposite side of the plane and hauled himself onto the curved top of the C-130. The tall bearded merc spotted the fleeing figure of the fourth patrolman and snap-aimed his F-1 submachine gun.

Caine raised the barrel a bit high and to the left of his intended target. He guessed the man's route toward the Jeep correctly and the guy rushed right into a stream of

9-mm rounds from Caine's Aussie subgun. Bullets hammered the gunman's head and shoulders, splintering collarbone and pulverizing the guy's skull like an eggshell hit by a battle-ax.

"That's all of em!" O'Neal shouted as he slithered back through the trapdoor into the cockpit.

"More coming our way!" Caine corrected from his perch at the roof of the C-130. "Two more Jeeps! And one of them has a mounted machine gun!"

"Jesus!" Kip rasped. "Those bastards are gonna shoot the shit outa my plane!"

"If they manage that we'll probably all be dead anyway!" O'Neal commented as he handed Kip his F-1 subgun. "Just in case you need it."

"Thanks," the pilot said without enthusiasm.

"If things get too hot for you," O'Nead added, "we'll understand if you have to take off."

"Don't worry about me, mate," Kip replied. "Go do your job and g'd luck."

The four Hard Corps mercs rushed from the plane to the ridge. Wentworth tossed his F-1 to Fanelli and took an FAL assault rifle from a slain patrolman. Caine held on to his submachine gun, but also grabbed another FAL rifle from the hands of a corpse. O'Neal carried the fourth F-1 blaster from the cargo hold of the plane.

They watched the enemy Jeeps approach as they took up position along the ridge, using the natural formation as shelter, similar to a wall of sandbags. The enemy vehicles didn't rush forward, obviously fearful that they'd wind up like the first group of roving patrolmen. O'Neal inspected the enemy through the lenses of his binoculars.

Each Jeep carried three men: a driver, a shooter, and a lookout with field glasses. As Caine had noticed before, one of the vehicles was equipped with a .30-caliber machine gun mounted at the rear with the barrel across the top of the windshield. The situation was bad enough, but the sound of big rotor blades slicing air told them things had just taken a drastic turn for the worse.

Every Vietnam veteran recognizes the roar of a helicopter. The sound never really goes away. It comes back in dreams, usually the kind from which one awakes in a cold sweat with a pounding heart and a dry mouth. The enemy chopper wasn't the product of a nightmare and it was closing in fast.

"Jim, take the chopper!" O'Neal ordered. "Steve, go for the Jeep with the thirty-cal. Joe gets the other rig. I'll try to draw their fire."

"Let me do it, Captain," Fanelli urged.

"I already told you what to do," O'Neal replied. "And you'd all better do it the right the first time 'cause we won't live to get a second chance."

O'Neal darted along the ridge to the incline at the end. The other mercs spread out to prevent giving the enemy a single easy target clustered together. They held their fire even as the roar of the helicopter rotors drew closer and the powerful draft of the spinning blades caused dust to whirl up from the ground above the ridge.

The Hard Corps commander sucked in a deep breath and held it. Then he swung around the edge of the ridge and fired his F-1 submachine gun. He sprayed an indiscriminate volley of 9-mm rounds at the two approaching Jeeps. O'Neal glimpsed the Lynx 'copter as the craft hovered overhead. A figure was stationed at the mouth of the sliding doors to the carriage, supported by a safety belt and armed with a mounted .30-caliber machine gun.

The chopper blasted a vicious salvo of high-powered projectiles at O'Neal's position. Bullets ripped into the ridge as O'Neal ducked low and clenched his teeth. Ricochets whined against rocks. One bullet tugged O'Neal's collar and slashed a burning gash along the nape of his neck. The maniacal sound of angry missiles buzzed over O'Neal's head as the machine gun continued to bellow with metallic chatter.

Wentworth, Caine, and Fanelli took action in unison, the three men acting as a single fighting unit. Wentworth put the stock of an FAL to his shoulder and raised the

barrel high even before he spotted the helicopter. The front
sight found the windscreen to the whirlybird and Wentworth put his eye to the rear sights to zero in on his target.

Caine used the ridge as a bench rest for his rifle and
rapidly aimed at the Jeep with the .30-caliber death machine. Fanelli hastily pointed his F-1 subgun at the other
Jeep, aware the vehicle was still beyond accurate range of
the Aussie blaster. All three men opened fire simultaneously.

A three-round burst from Wentworth's FAL punched a
trio of holes in the Plexiglas of the helicopter. The 7.62-
mm slugs drilled into the chest of the chopper pilot. The
dead man slumped against the cyclic controls and his feet
slid off the rudders. The Lynx swung into a wild arc to the
right. The violent motion shifted the dead weight of the
pilot and the direction of the copter changed as the body
moved against the controls.

The panicked machine gunner screamed as he fumbled
with the safety belt. The 'copter spun about and started to
head back toward the enemy stronghold, but it was losing
altitude fast. The chopper descended at an awkward angle,
the rotor blades striking earth first. The violent impact bent
metal. The nose smashed into the ground, and the helicopter crunched like a beer can in a trash compacter. The fuel
tank erupted and the Lynx exploded into a mass of metal
shards and flaming petrol.

Caine had fired his FAL on semiauto for greater accuracy. The marksman mercenary saw the face of the Jeep
driver in the sights of his rifle a split second before he put a
bullet in it. The copper-jacketed slug pierced the windshield and smashed into the bridge of the driver's nose.
Caine quickly raised the sights slightly and triggered two
more shots. The bullets struck the FUI gunner behind the
.30-caliber weapon. The man flung his arms apart as if
trying to embrace death. He succeeded. His corpse
slumped across the mounted machine gun.

The Jeep swerved out of control and swung toward the
other vehicle, nearly colliding with it. The terrified FUL

flunky who'd been acting as lookout for the first Jeep decided to bail out. He jumped from the vehicle and landed in the path of the second Jeep. The driver didn't have time to avoid him. Tires rolled across the man's lower back, crushing his spine.

Fanelli had fired his F-1 submachine gun at the second Jeep with little hope of causing any real damage, but the vehicle had actually rushed forward to avoid being hit by the other rig. It ran right into the field of fire from Fanelli's weapon. Nine-millimeter slugs punched into the radiator and raked the tires of the Jeep. The driver fought the wheel, trying to control the twin blowouts of his front tires. The guy riding shotgun was thrown from the vehicle and hit the ground with a bone-crunching splat.

The other two FUL goons brought the crippled Jeep to a halt, jumped out, and crouched behind it for shelter. Fanelli yanked the pin from a "flash-bang" grenade and hurled it at the vehicle. The blaster hit the ground and rolled under the Jeep. The explosion literally lifted the vehicle before smashing it down on the enemy gunsels.

"Now that's what I call whittling down the odds," O'Neal announced, delighted with the efficiency of his men. "But we've still got a lot of bastards left to take care of before this mission is finished."

"So let's pay a house call on Glover and his goons," Fanelli replied as he climbed over the ridge. "And I think we can use one of the Jeeps driven by the first batch of scumbags to welcome us to the base."

"Figure we'll just drive up to the front door?" Wentworth asked, clucking his tongue with disgust.

"Naw," Fanelli said as he reached for the pack of C-3 plastic explosives on his back. "I got somethin' else in mind."

CHAPTER 15

"GODDAMN IT, THOR!" Harold Glover snarled at his chief enforcer. "What the hell has happened to our bloody security around here?"

"A helicopter's down, Harry..." Thor Ornjarta began lamely. The big muscle-bound Swede was as dumbfounded and alarmed as his boss. "But I sent a dozen men to take care of it. They were packing enough firepower to wipe out a battalion!"

"I doubt if they had a battalion in that plane," Jean-Claude LeTrec commented bitterly, staring out the window of Glover's immaculate office to watch the wreckage of the Lynx helicopter burn. "But they were certainly too much for your people to handle."

"We'll see about that," Thor growled, offended by the Frenchman's remark.

"You can let us know about the outcome later," LeTrec replied with a sneer. He turned to three young Asian bodyguards who had accompanied him on his assignment. *"Wumen li'ke jyow-yau dzow leh!"*

"Sher, Lee-Trek Syaun-sheng," the Golden Triangle Triad enforcers replied, bowing to the Frenchman.

165

"What's this conversation all about?" Glover demanded. He didn't understand enough Chinese to know what he was ordering in a Cantonese restaurant, and he didn't like people speaking a language he couldn't understand.

"*Au revoir,*" LeTrec told Glover with an exaggerated bow. "It is now every man for himself. *Oui?*"

LeTrec and his trio of bodyguards marched from the office. Kwan Li Que watched them leave, but the Singapore Triad gangster didn't follow the Frenchman's example. He turned to Glover.

"Jean-Claude and his people are going to try to leave now," Kwan declared. "Probably thinks he can fly out of here in his helicopter."

"You're not going, Kwan?" Glover inquired with surprise. He didn't think Kwan was the type to remain in a dangerous situation. The Chinese gangster certainly had no reason to feel any loyalty toward Glover.

"Not by helicopter," Kwan replied. "One of your craft was already shot down and it was armed with a machine gun. I don't see that LeTrec is apt to do any better."

"You think you can walk out?" Glover asked.

"Walk from the outback?" Kwan smiled. "I think I'd rather take my chances with whoever's attacking us."

"Thor." Glover turned to his chief enforcer. "See if you can get some spare weapons and supply Mr. Kwan and his men with some decent firepower. Where's Daiku and his three bodyguards?"

"I saw them headed toward their quarters at the east wing," Thor answered. "I hope they don't intend to hide under their beds."

"Not the *yakuza,* I assure you," Kwan told him. "Daiku and his *kobun* are probably getting their swords ready. The *yakuza* still use cold steel more often than bullets. Don't underestimate them, either. At close quarters, a sword in the hands of an expert is as deadly as a gun."

"I don't care if the *yakuza* want to fight with stainless-steel baby rattles as long as they're on our side," Glover declared.

"Oh, Daiku will certainly fight with us against the invaders," Kwan assured the Aussie. "But, that's just a matter of self-interest. After the battle is over, Daiku may very well want your head as well."

"I'll worry about him later," Glover replied. "Once all of this is over." He remained confident in the strength of his forces.

The Hard Corps advanced toward the stronghold. Joe Fanelli sat behind the wheel of a Jeep and slowly drove the vehicle toward the heart of the enemy base. James Wentworth and Steve Caine moved along the sides of the Jeep on foot, FAL assault rifles held ready. O'Neal brought up the rear.

The mercenaries tried to remain partially camouflaged by columns of black smoke from the burning 'copter wreckage. They were targets for the enemy, but they could see little of the activity within the stronghold. More than a dozen young men and women had ventured timidly from the wooden billets. None of them went beyond easy reach of a doorway.

Fifteen FUL gunmen had emerged from the main house. Two of them fired some submachine-gun rounds over the heads of the curious young people. The kids took the warning to heart and retreated back inside the barracks. This suited the Hard Corps as well as the cult. None of them wanted the teenagers in the way during combat.

In addition to the enemy outside the buildings, several gunmen were stationed at windows and on the roof of the main house. The Hard Corps also noticed four men headed toward one of the helicopters at the pad near the motor pool. One of the men was a small swarthy Caucasian and the others were Asians.

"You sure you want to do this, Joe?" O'Neal asked Fanelli.

"Hell, no," Fanelli replied as he hunched low in the driver's seat. "I don't *want* to do it, but it was my idea, after all."

"He doesn't get them very often," Wentworth commented.

"Everybody get ready," O'Neal ordered. He was in no mood for listening to any bickering, but he knew his men were too professional to screw around in such a critical situation. "Joe's gonna need plenty of cover fire."

"Okay," Fanelli announced. "I'm ready, I'm set, and I'm goin' . . ."

He stomped on the gas and turned the steering wheel sharply to the right. The Jeep bolted forward and swung in a wide arc toward the motor pool and helicopter pad. Several enemy bullets struck the Jeep. The windshield shattered and broken glass shrouded Fanelli as he crouched under the dashboard, a leg turned awkwardly to keep a foot on the gas pedal.

Fanelli had attached a cord to the framework under the passenger's seat. The rope was secured with a carabiner and another "D" style snap link was attached to the free end. Fanelli snapped the carabiner on the steering wheel and locked it in place. The rope was taut and would help keep the wheel from moving too far to the left.

The merc let up on the gas and allowed the car to roll on its own momentum. Enemy bullets had punctured at least one tire, but that wasn't important. The car could roll along on all four hubs and still reach its target . . . more or less. Close enough would be good enough, since Fanelli had rigged half a pound of C-3 in the backseat. The detonator was hooked up to a wristwatch with an alarm setting and it was going to buzz in less than a minute.

Fanelli shoved open the door and dived out. He hit the ground in a rapid shoulder roll. Pain lanced through him as he landed on the shoulder that had been shot up by buckshot back in California. A bullet bit into the earth near his tumbling form. It had been fired by a sniper on the roof. Wentworth's FAL responded to the gunman's weapon and the sniper screamed, plunging headfirst from his perch.

The Jeep continued to roll toward the helipad as the 'copter containing LeTrec and his Triad bodyguards started to rise. The helicopter climbed six feet in the air before the Jeep passed under it and the C-3 charge exploded.

The blast was monstrous and the upward force sent the helicopter into a violent tailspin. The chopper whirled out of control. LeTrec had only a few ghastly moments remaining in his life to realize that he should have chosen to stay and fight with the others, before the chopper pivoted into the side of the house. The fuel tank exploded and the whirlybird blew into a savage nova, caving in a wall of Glover's headquarters building. LeTrec and his bodyguards virtually disintegrated in the awesome blast.

The exploding helicopter joined the C-3 explosion to wreak havoc across the helicopter pad and the motor pool. A destructive chain reaction occurred. The third and last enemy helicopter was also bombarded by the blast. Chopper Number Three exploded with a fury that matched the other whirlybird blast.

The third explosion sent jets of flaming fuel across the great drums containing fuel for the helicopters and land vehicles. The big tanks exploded and flaming gasoline spewed in all directions. Burning petrol splashed the trucks and buses that remained in the motor pool. No one could reach the fiery vehicles to put out the blaze; no one even tried. One by one, more fuel tanks blew each rig to pieces.

Fiery fuel was also dousing the house. The brick structure might have been spared any serious damage by the flames if the Triad chopper hadn't smashed into the wall. But now, fire spat into the interior of the house and rapidly spread, because no one could take time to try to stop it.

The tactic had worked far better than the Hard Corps could have expected. Fanelli's car-bomb stunt had resulted in the greatest example of the domino theory since Southeast Asia. The headquarters was half-destroyed and the rest was burning up. The majority of the Fellowship of Ultimate Living thugs were already dead, slain by the explosions and the skillfully delivered cover fire by the other three Hard Corps mercenaries.

Both sides of the conflict were running low on ammunition and the Hard Corps had reloaded their weapons with the last magazines. Wentworth had already burned up his FAL ammo and was forced to draw his pistol. Caine was also out of rifle ammo, so he discarded the empty FAL and switched to the F-1 submachine gun he carried. O'Neal had only a few rounds left for his Aussie blaster. Only Fanelli had a full magazine in his subgun.

The enemy were greater in numbers, but largely inexperienced in combat situations. The Hard Corps' bold tactics had stunned and demoralized the FUL forces and none of Glover's men came close to matching the skills of the mercenaries. The situation was rather like a pack of wild dogs pitted against four tigers. As the number of dogs declined, the odds went up in favor of the big cats.

The Hard Corps reached the house—or what was left of it. They lobbed concussion grenades through windows, the front door, and the enormous gap in the west wing. The "flash-bang" explosions erupted and the Hard Corps charged inside with weapons at the ready.

Caine and Fanelli entered through the missing wall. They slipped through the side with the least amount of flame barring their path and plunged into a long hallway. Three FUL hoods staggered through the corridor, choking from smoke inhalation. Fanelli promptly hosed them down with his F-1 subgun.

The pair followed the corridor and located a metal freezer door in the kitchen. The setup was much the same as in the California base. Fanelli quickly rigged some C-3 and, with little ceremony, blew open the door. Caine stood guard in the kitchen while Fanelli descended the stairs of the hidden basement to liberate the half-starved and tortured youths in the cellblocks under the house. Fanneli's task was grim, but not dangerous, since all the guards stationed at the cellblock had been called from their post to join in the fight.

Caine, meanwhile, found himself in a very different situation.

Kwan Li Que and his three Triad bodyguards rushed

into the kitchen. The Singapore outlaws were seeking a safe exit from the burning house and the kitchen had seemed a likely place for a door to freedom. The Triad had grabbed what weapons they could find from the bodies of slain FUL enforcers and charged into the room, unaware of Caine's presence.

The Triad responded immediately to the unexpected encounter with the merc. Kwan raised a pistol. His chief protector dropped into a kneeling stance and pointed a British Sterling submachine gun at Caine while the other two Triad thugs moved to the left and advanced in a crouched position with knives in their fists.

Caine dealt with the greatest threat first. His F-1 submachine gun spat orange flame and slammed four 9-mm slugs into the stomach and chest of the Triad hood with the British chatter-gun. Two parabellums struck Kwan just above the breastbone. The Triad ringleader spun about and fell to his knees as the corpse of his bodyguard hit the floor beside him.

The knife-wielding killers closed in before Caine could shift the aim of his weapon to deal with them. The closest thug swung a roundhouse kick to Caine's F-1 and struck the submachine gun from the mercenary's hands. The Triad slashed his combat Bowie knife at Caine's face. The mercenary dodged the enemy blade and jumped away from his opponent, instinctively reaching for the survival knife on his hip.

The Triad thug snap-kicked Caine in the abdomen. The merc grunted and started to double up from the blow, but managed to draw his knife from its sheath. His opponent delivered a deadly knife stroke at the side of Caine's neck, blade aimed at the carotid artery. The Hard Corps pro raised his left forearm to ward off the blow. Sharp steel sliced Caine's sleeve and cut a deep gash above his wrist.

Pain streaked up Caine's arm as he backed away from the Triad knife artist. Blood soaked Caine's left sleeve, but the fingers of his left hand still worked and he didn't think any serious damage to muscles and tendons had occurred.

"Wang pu-tan!" the man with the Bowie knife spat as he slowly waved his bloodstained blade in small circles.

The other knife-wielding Singapore thug moved to the right of his partner. He held an army bayonet in an overhand grip, eight-inch blade jutting from the bottom of his fist. The Triad pair smiled, confident that Caine would be helpless if they attacked in unison.

Caine realized he was facing difficult odds. The Triad thugs were obviously experienced knife-fighters and trained in martial arts. Yet Caine sensed a weakness in his opponents. The Triad hoods clearly thought their American opponent presented no real threat without a gun. If they underestimated Caine, they might just make a fatal mistake. At least, that's what Caine hoped.

The mercenary flashed the six-inch blade of his survival knife at the Triad with the Bowie. The man stepped back to stand clear of the merc's knife and raised his own to counter the attack. However, Caine's move was a feint. He guessed how the Bowie-wielding hood would react and hoped he would be correct about the guy with the bayonet as well.

The second Triad hood lunged with his bayonet, weapon aimed to the left of Caine's rib cage. A bayonet is designed for stabbing, not cutting. Caine anticipated this tactic. He dodged the bayonet thrust and slashed the blade of his survival knife across the hood's wrist. The man cried out in pain as the bayonet fell to the floor.

The other knife artist attacked as Caine grabbed the wounded man by the hair and pulled the man forward in between himself and his opponent. The Bowie knife struck flesh and split bone. The Triad knife artist gasped with surprise and alarm as he realized he had plunged his weapon into the chest of his fellow thug.

The wounded man screamed and Caine held on to his hair to thrust the dying man's head forward. He butted the thug's skull into the face of the other knife fighter. Caine shoved the dying man into his other opponent and shifted the survival knife to his left hand. Caine's right drew the

Browning automatic from his belt and thumbed off the safety catch.

The surviving Triad thug shoved his dead partner aside and held his bloodied knife for further combat. He stared at the pistol in Caine's fist and realized he was dead even before the mercenary squeezed the trigger. A 115-grain parabellum shattered the Triad hood's forehead and tore through his brain as if it were a rotten potato.

Kwan Li Que sat on the floor with his back against a wall. The Singapore gangster knew he was dying. There wasn't much blood on his suit jacket and white shirt, but he felt his life ebbing away. Internal bleeding, he figured. Without medical aid he'd be dead in half an hour.

Kwan still had his pistol, but his vision was already blurred and hazy. There seemed to be no point in trying to kill Caine. Kwan was a business manager for the Triad, not a soldier. He'd never been much good with weapons or fighting. Kwan decided the gun would serve him better as a method of speeding his own death.

He jammed the barrel into his mouth and poked the muzzle upward. His teeth tapped nervously along the metal and the taste of the pistol filled his tongue. The muzzle was pressed against the roof of his mouth. It was uncomfortable and Kwan felt a little foolish. But he didn't have to feel foolish for long. He squeezed the trigger and his skull exploded.

James Wentworth heard voices as he approached Glover's office. The mercenary lieutenant held his Browning pistol in both hands and kicked in the door. A long steel blade flashed through the opening. Wentworth jerked away from the sword. The blade struck the wood frame of the doorway, the sharp edge biting deep.

Wentworth saw the fierce features of the *yakuza* thug who wielded the sword. The mercenary's pistol roared and the man's face vanished in a glob of crimson. The *yakuza* hood fell to the floor of the office. The sword remained lodged in the door frame.

Daiku and the other two *yakuza* bodyguards stood inside the office. Athletic young Japanese with strong bodies and rigid faces, they carried no firearms, although each held a *katana* samurai sword in his fists. The two *kobun* enforcers stood in front of their leader, determined to protect him with their lives if necessary.

"I don't imagine there's much point in telling you fellas to surrender," Wentworth remarked.

The two *kobun* answered by attacking the merc lieutenant. One charged with his sword held overhead while the other poised his *katana* at chest level and rapidly shuffled forward. Wentworth shot the first man, quickly pumping two 9-mm rounds through the *kobun's* chest. The swordsman staggered, but kept coming.

Wentworth shot him again. Blood formed a wide scarlet patch on the Asian's shirt, yet the man still stumbled forward and swung his *katana*. Wentworth sidestepped and narrowly avoided the descending ribbon of razor-sharp steel. The *kobun* collapsed face-first to the floor, dead before he hit the surface.

The other swordsman swung his *katana*, blade aimed at Wentworth's wrists in an attempt to chop off the merc's hands and render the pistol useless. The mercenary drew back from the attack and the sword struck the steel frame of his Browning. The force knocked the pistol from Wentworth's grasp.

The swordsman raised his blade for another stroke. Wentworth quickly grabbed the hilt of the *katana* stuck in the door frame. He yanked the blade free as the *yakuza* hood swung his weapon. Blades clashed as Wentworth blocked the attack with the other sword.

The *yakuza* thug was surprised by Wentworth's tactic, but assumed it had been a fluke. The mercenary was an Occidental and certainly not skilled in *kendo*. The swordsman struck out again, attempting a cut to Wentworth's neck. The merc blocked with the flat of his sword and pushed the enemy blade aside. Wentworth suddenly delivered a fast backhand sweep. His sword slashed the *kobun's* throat. The thug staggered backward, a fountain of blood released by the terrible wound.

Daiku's eyes hardened as he watched his last bodyguard drop dead before his eyes. The *yakuza* leader stared at Wentworth. The merc held the *katana* in a proper two-hand grip, his feet in a balanced stance. Daiku nodded and raised his own sword.

"Shall we finish this?" he inquired.

"One way or the other," Wentworth agreed.

They squared off and slowly advanced, each trying to determine the strategy of the other. Daiku was clearly a far better swordsman than his overzealous *kobun* had been. Wentworth decided to let his opponent make the first move.

Daiku didn't disappoint him. The *yakuza* gangster swung a short overhead stroke and suddenly altered the attack to a roundhouse swing. Wentworth blocked with his blade and tried to slide the point forward to stab his opponent in the face or throat. Daiku pushed his sword upward and shoved Wentworth's blade aside.

The *yakuza* hood's sword slashed a rapid cut to Wentworth's belly. The merc retreated from the blade, but the tip still raked his abdomen. Pain gripped Wentworth's belly as blood oozed from the shallow cut. Daiku's blade swung again. Steel clashed as Wentworth blocked the stroke.

Daiku swung a kick to Wentworth's ribs and knocked the merc lieutenant off balance. Wentworth landed against a wall and barely managed to parry another sword stroke from his opponent. He pushed himself away from the wall and Daiku swung a low slash at Wentworth's groin. The merc swatted the attack aside with the flat of his blade and thrust the steel point at Daiku's chest.

The *yakuza* gangster dodged the attack and swung a cross-body sword stroke at Wentworth's head. The merc ducked under the whirling steel blade and slashed his *katana* across Daiku's belly. Purple and green intestines poured from the man's slit abdomen. Daiku staggered backward, uttering a low grunt although his eyes were filled with pain.

Wentworth raised his sword again and delivered a powerful stroke to the side of his opponent's neck. Sharp steel sliced through muscle and bone. Daiku's head dropped to the floor and tumbled across the room. The *yakuza* hood's decapitated corpse fell a split second later, blood gushing from the stump of his neck.

"*Sayonara,*" Wentworth remarked as he gazed down at the headless body.

CHAPTER 16

HAROLD GLOVER AND Thor Ornjarta were in the library. The room, in addition to having bookcases and tables with chairs for readers involved in research, also had leather arm chairs, a well-stocked bar, and a wide-screen television set. As with any room that Glover spent much time in, a large mirror was mounted on a wall.

"I still think we should stay and fight," Thor complained, canting a double-barrel shotgun across a thickly muscled shoulder. "We can still win . . ."

"You don't think, period," Glover snapped, nervously tapping the barrel of a Beretta against his palm. He was not accustomed to carrying a gun and the weapon felt awkward and unfamiliar in his hands. "Our defenses have been broken. That means your men have already failed to stop the invaders. They hit them with the best they had and it wasn't good enough. What the hell makes you think we can turn the tide of battle now?"

"But I—" Thor began lamely.

"Just shut up," Glover told him. "We're going to need some emergency cash to get out of the country. Might be bloody expensive since we can't take the chance of using commercial airlines."

"Where are we going, Harry?" Thor inquired with a frown.

"Europe, I suppose," Glover answered as he moved around a large wooden globe to approach a set of bookshelves flush against the wall.

"Europe?" Thor asked with dismay. "I can't go back to Europe. The police will arrest me."

"That's your problem," Glover replied, pulling the bookcase. It creaked forward like a door to reveal a hidden closet containing a large metal safe. "After we get settled somewhere, I'll get some cash from the Swiss account and we'll figure out what to do."

An unexpected blow between the shoulder blades propelled Glover forward into the safe. His forehead struck the hard metal surface. Thor seized Glover from behind, gripping his boss at the back of the neck with one hand and striking the Beretta from Glover's grasp with a blow from the twin barrels of his shotgun.

"You think you're going to use me for protection until you get out of Australia and then leave me stranded to face the police alone?" Thor hissed as he discarded the shotgun to grab Glover's neck with both hands.

"No . . ." Glover rasped, his throat constricted by powerful fingers. It was the only word he could utter before his breath was cut off by the strangler's grip.

"You use everyone and throw them away!" Thor bellowed. He lifted Glover's feet from the floor as he held the smaller man's neck with squeezing fingers. "I know your game better than anyone!"

Glover struggled helplessly. He tugged at Thor's wrists and clawed the larger man's hands with his fingernails, but Thor's grip remained firmly around his neck. Glover's feet lashed air as he kicked wildly above the library floor. The back of a heel hit Thor in the abdomen, but the big Swede didn't even grunt as he continued to throttle Glover, hanging the Australian cult leader with his bare hands.

Thor's powerful fingers dug deeper into Glover's throat. The victim's resistance grew weaker until Glover's body went limp. Thor still held on to the other man's neck. He wanted to make certain Glover wasn't just pretending to be dead.

O'Neal, meanwhile, had entered the library. The Hard Corps commander sure as hell hadn't expected to see the enemy killing each other. O'Neal could only guess what Glover and his pet gorilla were fighting over, and he didn't really care. If the dumb bastards wanted to make his job easier, that was fine with him.

The merc captain pointed his F-1 chopper at the pair, but he held his fire. Gunning down unarmed opponents in cold blood wasn't O'Neal's style. Glover and Thor richly deserved immediate execution, in O'Neal's opinion, but he was still reluctant to carry out the sentence in this situation.

Thor saw O'Neal via the corner of an eye and immediately reacted to the threat of the mercenary's submachine gun. O'Neal suddenly regretted his reluctance to open fire when Thor hurled the closest object available at the mercenary. Glover's body sailed into O'Neal like an oversized rag doll. The limp form struck with considerable force, due to Thor's mighty throw. O'Neal's battle-honed reflexes helped him dodge the unorthodox projectile, but Glover collided with his right elbow and the impact jarred his hand from the trigger mechanism of the subgun.

"Shit!" O'Neal rasped as the F-1 slipped from his grasp.

Thor charged forward, massive hands poised like claws, fingers arched as if prepared to tear O'Neal limb from limb. Thor might indeed be capable of literally accomplishing such a feat, O'Neal realized. The merc recalled how the big Swede had easily snapped the steel links to a pair of handcuffs. O'Neal didn't relish the idea of taking on Thor in hand-to-hand combat.

The merc jumped backward to get some distance from Thor. His hand streaked to the Browning automatic in his belt as the red-haired hulk drew closer. O'Neal relied on years of training in combat handgun shooting and the experience of hundreds of actual gunfights. His reflexes acted faster than conscious thought. O'Neal drew the pistol, snapped off the safety as he pointed the weapon, and immediately squeezed the trigger.

O'Neal fired three rounds. He automatically took a step back and dropped to one knee as he triggered the pistol as rapidly as his finger and the mechanism of the weapon allowed. All three parabellums burrowed into Thor's barrel chest, but the big man didn't fall. Blood and saliva dribbled from Thor's open mouth and his eyes were wild with pain and rage.

The mercenary's finger began to press the trigger of the Browning, prepared to fire another 9-mm round into his monstrous opponent. Thor uttered an ugly growling sound as more blood bubbled from his lips. The big bastard had been shot through both lungs. At last, his knees buckled and Thor fell to all fours.

O'Neal sighed with relief and slowly rose, Browning still pointed at the wounded figure of his brutish opponent. A soft groan drew O'Neal's attention toward Harold Glover. The cult leader stirred slightly as he began to recover consciousness. O'Neal shifted the aim of his pistol to point the muzzle between Glover and Thor in case either man presented a threat.

Suddenly, Thor bolted up from the floor and charged like an enraged bull. O'Neal turned sharply and tried to aim his pistol at the brute's bowed head. Thor crashed into O'Neal before the merc could trigger his weapon. Both men staggered across the room and fell against a table.

The Browning pistol fell from O'Neal's hands as Thor shoved him across the tabletop and seized the mercenary's throat. O'Neal quickly slapped his open palms into the big man's ears. Thor roared with fresh agony as his eardrums exploded, but he still held on to O'Neal's throat.

The merc's windpipe felt as if it was locked in a steel vise. His head felt like a pressure cooker and his vision was blotted out by bursts of white lights popping inside his skull. O'Neal's strength was fading rapidly and he knew he had to act quickly or die.

O'Neal's hands groped across Thor's broad face. He felt the man's cheeks and nose, then located his eyes. O'Neal jammed his thumbs hard. The Swede howled with pain and fear, aware O'Neal could pop his eyeballs from their sockets.

Thor released the merc's throat and knocked O'Neal's hands away from his face before the Hard Corps chief could blind him. The hulking savage quickly hammered a mallet-sized fist into O'Neal's chest. The merc gasped as the breath was driven from his lungs. O'Neal, amazed at Thor's endurance, wondered if the blow had cracked his sternum. He had never seen someone come back the way Thor had. He wondered how much longer Thor could last. Christ, the bastard had stopped three 9-mm parabellums with his chest, but he still seemed as strong as a bull buffalo and just as tough.

O'Neal pushed himself from the table and swung a right cross to Thor's face. Knuckles connected hard and O'Neal's fist stung from the blow, but Thor's head barely moved. The big man seized O'Neal's shirtfront and raised him from the table.

O'Neal swung a kick to Thor's chest. The hulk's face contorted with pain, but Thor still lifted the mercenary as if O'Neal were a sack of potatoes. He hauled the merc captain overhead. O'Neal kept swinging, kicking at Thor's chest and face and prying at the Swede's fingers to try to loosen his opponent's grip. Nothing worked.

Thor suddenly hurled O'Neal into a wall. The mercenary hit the surface hard and fell to the floor. Dazed, he looked up at the huge hoodlum through a hazy blur. Thor stepped forward and seemed to freeze in place. O'Neal tried to get up, but his body was wracked with pain. He tried to catch his breath and climb to his feet before Thor could close in and stomp him to death.

But Thor didn't move. He weaved slightly and crashed to the floor. The big man's body twitched slightly and lay still. O'Neal stared at Thor's lifeless eyes. The son of a bitch had finally run out of rage and realized he was dead. O'Neal slowly rose. He winced from a sharp pain in his side. Cracked rib, he figured. O'Neal knew he was lucky his back hadn't been broken.

"Freeze, you bas—bastard," an unsteady voice croaked.

O'Neal turned to find Harold Glover had regained consciousness. The Australian cult leader had also found O'Neal's Browning and held the pistol in an amateurish manner, which he'd probably learned from watching his goons. Glover held the gun in one fist and gripped his wrist with the other hand to steady his aim. In so doing, he failed to cradle the frame of the weapon with the free hand, making it a virtual variation of a one-hand grip. Not very accurate and even less stable, but the muzzle of the Browning was aimed at O'Neal and even a novice like Glover could hit a man-sized target only eight feet away. Also, Glover's strength was returning quickly now.

"You're finished, Glover," O'Neal told him, although he raised his empty hands to shoulder level. "Killing me won't change that."

"You?" Glover's eyes widened and the pistol trembled in his fist. "You were in California!"

"That's right," O'Neal replied as he stepped forward. He glanced down at the floor, hoping to locate his F-1 blaster, but the subgun lay behind Glover's feet. "We took out your outfit in the States and now we've come here to finish the job."

"Amazing," Glover said with astonishment. "You people aren't Federal agents or police officers, are you? You're nothing but a bunch of "hired gunmen." He paused, then smiled. "I know. It was Carol Henderson, wasn't it? She and her parents' committee."

"Does it matter?" O'Neal asked. He noticed the walnut stock of a weapon on the floor near the safe.

Glover clicked his tongue at O'Neal. "Ah, my stupid American friend. If you'd been smart you would have

come to me and made a deal. I would have paid you twice
—*three times*— what I'm sure you're getting from those
parents. I would have paid you just to walk away." He
paused. "We can still make a deal, if you prefer. I could
use your skills. I'd pay you well. It's not too late."

"We would never accept money from you," O'Neal answered, shuffling toward the globe. "Your money is too
dirty to touch. I've met a lot of slime, but I don't think I've
ever met anybody more disgusting than you."

"I know how to fire this!" Glover snapped, aware
O'Neal was up to something although he wasn't sure what
the merc's tactics might be. "Don't move a muscle. You
think you can outsmart *me?* I'm afraid that's impossible. I
created this cult. I organized the financial operations. *No*
one knows more than I do!!"

O'Neal stared at Glover. The bastard really believed
what he was saying! "You got the gun, genius," O'Neal
said with a shrug. "Sure taking you a long time to use it.
Takes a little guts to kill a man face-to-face. Is that the
problem? No guts?"

"I *will* kill you," Glover warned, but his tone suggested
he wasn't so sure himself. "Last chance, Mister Soldier!
Help me get out of here and I'll see you get your reward."

"Sure, I can help you," O'Neal replied as he slowly
lowered a hand and placed it on his aching side. "Your
bodyguard busted one of my ribs."

"It'll heal," Glover told him, pointing the Browning at
O'Neal's face. "Now how do I get out of here?"

"With a sheet over your head!" O'Neal yelled, hurling
himself to the floor.

Glover pulled the trigger. The Browning roared and a
9-mm round slashed air harmlessly almost a foot above
O'Neal's head as the mercenary dived for the carpet.
Glover wasn't accustomed to the recoil of a medium-cali-
ber pistol. His arm rose with the kick and Glover cursed
under his breath as he tried to adjust the aim.

O'Neal scrambled behind the globe and reached for the
stock of the weapon he'd noticed earlier. Another parabel-

lum round shrieked from the muzzle of the Browning as
Glover fired once more. The bullet smashed into the
wooden panels of the globe. The sphere rocked from the
impact of the 115-grain bullet. O'Neal tried to ignore
the near-miss as he reached for the weapon.

The gun was a side-by-side shotgun. Thor's gun.
O'Neal gathered up the weapon and slid across the floor
past the globe. He landed on his side. The cracked rib felt
like a knife blade under his lungs. O'Neal clenched his
teeth and pointed the twin barrels of the shotgun upward as
Glover turned to aim the Browning at the mercenary.

O'Neal squeezed a trigger to the shotgun. A burst of
buckshot bellowed from a barrel. The deadly blast of mer-
ciless pellets slammed into Glover's torso. The cult
leader's chest exploded in a burst of pink and scarlet pulp.
The force of the blast hurled Glover backwards across the
room. His body smashed into a wall and started to slide to
the floor. O'Neal figured the bloodied slab of meat was
already dead, but he fired the second barrel of the shotgun
to be sure Harold Glover would never get up again.

"Bill!" Wentworth called out as he entered the room.
The Hard Corps lieutenant glanced about at the bloody af-
termath of the battle. "Looks like you've been busy. Are
you all right?"

"I've felt better," O'Neal admitted, wincing. "How we
doin'?"

"We won," Wentworth explained as he helped O'Neal to
his feet. "Fanelli found a bunch of kids in a cellblock in the
basement and they're explaining to the kids in the billets
what Glover really had in store for them. A few are taking
it hard, but most of 'em don't seem too surprised. Guess
they were already suspicious."

"Great . . ." O'Neal hissed as pain lanced his side. He
felt his ribs. Nothing had caved in so he didn't have to
worry about puncturing a lung with a splinter of his own
rib. "Guess we'd better get the hell out of here and contact
the Aussies to mop up what's left."

"Carol Henderson will certainly be pleased," Wentworth commented.

"She'll be busy," O'Neal replied as he allowed Wentworth to help him limp from the library. "Carol's involved in drug rehab. A lot of these kids are gonna have a problem kicking the habits Glover forced on them. You can bet Carol will be right in the middle of that project."

"I guess we'll need to find another project ourselves," Wentworth remarked as they moved into the hallway.

"Yeah, but don't sound so glum," O'Neal commented. "There's always another war to fight, isn't there?"